# REAL ROMANCE

by

Ginny Baird

REAL ROMANCE
by
Ginny Baird

Published by
Winter Wedding Press

Copyright © 2012
Ginny Baird
Trade Paperback
ISBN 978-0-9858225-1-4

Cover by Darleen Dixon

Originally published in paperback by
Zebra Books
Kensington Publishing Corp.
Copyright © 2000

# About the Author

From the time that she could talk, romance author Ginny Baird was making up stories, much to the delight -- and consternation -- of her family and friends. By grade school, she'd turned that inclination into a talent, whereby her teacher allowed her to write and produce plays, rather than write boring book reports. Ginny continued writing throughout college, where she contributed articles to her literary campus weekly, then later pursued a career managing international projects with the US State Department.

Ginny's held an assortment of jobs, including school teacher, freelance fashion model, and greeting card writer, and has published more than ten works of fiction and optioned nine screenplays. She's additionally published short stories, nonfiction and poetry, and admits to being a true romantic at heart.

Ginny is the author of bestselling novels *The Sometime Bride* and *Real Romance*, and has just launched her "Girls on the Go" series, which premiered with *Santa Fe Fortune*. She's a member of Romance Writers of America (RWA), the RWA Published Authors Network (PAN), and the RWA Published Authors Special Interest Chapter (PASIC).

Ginny lives with her family in Tidewater, Virginia. When she's not writing, Ginny enjoys cooking, biking and just about any word game, including crossword puzzles and Scrabble. She loves hearing from her readers by email at GinnyBairdRomance@gmail.com and can also be found on Facebook http://www.facebook.com/GinnyBairdRomance and Twitter @GinnyBaird.

# REAL ROMANCE

## by

## Ginny Baird

# Chapter One

"So, what do you think?"

Marie McCloud opened her eyes wide and blinked. She saw bright blue eyes looking into hers, and a glacier-melting smile. What did she think, indeed.

When she'd walked into the spectacle shop nearly an hour ago, her vision had been so fuzzy she'd barely been able to make out the blue shirt and slacks the optician wore, let alone his muscular build. Now that she could focus, Marie was all too aware that the smooth-as-silk southern baritone was coming from a stunning specimen of masculinity.

She adjusted the frames on her nose and felt herself blush.

"Fine," was all she could manage to say through her clogged throat. "I'll take you. I mean, them."

Marie lifted a hand to wipe the tiny beads of sweat gathering at her hairline, thinking it was awfully hot in here for October. November. What the heck month was it, anyway?

"Well, they suit you," he said, sending the room spinning, as he leaned forward with an appraising smile.

The frames did look good with her chestnut brown hair. She was really quite attractive. Gorgeous, some would say. In an understated way, that a lesser man might think of as mousy. But David Lake knew better. He'd hooked up with more than one soft-spoken brunette in his lifetime. And every one of them had a fiery furnace burning beneath that creamy, cool exterior.

Something in her big, brown eyes told David that Marie McCloud was no different. The only question was, did she know it?

David checked his watch, then glanced back at her lovely face, trying hard not to be obvious. There was something in the delicate curve of her cheek, the long, porcelain line of her neck, the richly dark tendrils, spiraling recklessly from her pulled-back hair.

"Have any plans for lunch?" he asked, his lips racing with the thought that had barely formed in his brain.

She looked him up and down and blinked again, her color going all pink and cinnamony.

His hair was sandy and cropped short. Parted neatly on the side. He looked less like an optician and more like... a lifeguard. Marie froze momentarily at the thought of him administering mouth-to-mouth.

"I, ah..."

David glanced nervously over his shoulder to see if Caroline, his boss, had been listening. She'd have his head for certain. Socializing with the clients. Last time he'd done it, he'd nearly lost his job. Didn't help that Cindy had threatened to smash a whole wall of designer frames when he'd finally called things off.

"Can't." Marie sprang from her seat like a frightened cat. "Oh my gosh," she said, studying the clock on the wall, "twelve-thirty! Gotta be getting back."

"I'm sure they'll understand at..." David waited, hoping she'd fill in the blank.

"Books & Bistro," Marie added hastily, making her way toward the counter and digging for the checkbook in her purse. She bit into her bottom lip, realizing what she'd just done.

So now he knew where she worked, David thought, ringing up her purchase. And it was right around the corner.

"Well," he said, eyeing the soft curves of her body beneath her figure-hugging sweater dress. "You couldn't have overrun your lunch hour by that much. Surely, they won't throw the book at you."

Marie looked up at a smile brighter than sunlight on freshly fallen snow. His crisply pressed shirt did little to disguise his delectable shoulders and broad chest. The flat plane of his stomach that ran in a flawless line right down to...

Book! The only books Marie should have thrown at her were all those romances she wasted so much time reading. Silly escapism. Nothing like that ever happened in real life.

His hand grazed hers as he passed over a fabric-covered glasses case. "Hope you have better luck this time."

Marie laid down her checkbook and steadied herself against the counter. What was it in those clear, blue eyes that turned her knees to butter?

"With the glasses," David said, thinking he'd read her look. She'd been burned, that's what it was.

Bad luck with men, in a town like Covesville where the women outnumbered the male population ten to one, was commonplace in these parts. And David, he realized with a sense of shame, was partially to blame for those dismal statistics. He'd had plenty of opportunity with women. Plenty of opportunity, that was, to break their hearts. But why in the world was he thinking of that now?

Not that David ever tried to hurt anybody intentionally. It just appeared to be an unhappy by-product of his becoming romantically involved. He couldn't seem to help it. No matter what he tried to tell himself, there was something about the notion of a woman demanding a commitment that made him want to cut and run.

"Thanks," she said, accepting the paperwork along with the receipt. "I'll try to be more careful."

Then David realized she was running out on him. He panicked and stepped in front of her, blocking her sumptuous body with his broad frame.

"Is there something I've forgotten?" she asked, looking up with doe-like eyes.

It took every ounce of his strength not to reach out and touch her. Not to find some excuse to...

David's hands were halfway to the edge of her wire frames before he realized what he was doing and stopped short.

"Just wanted to make sure the fit's okay," David said, his hands motioning in the air surrounding Marie's shoulders.

Marie smiled shyly. "Couldn't be better," she answered, her voice an inexplicable squeak.

Up close, he smelled as good as he looked. All musky and exotic, like some forbidden, sensual body oil sold in the back room of a Moroccan bazaar.

Marie shook her head, thinking she should have known better than to read the last chapter of *Arabian Lust* over a donut at her ten-thirty coffee break. There was something about this man, this tall hunk of masculinity, that made her feel very female. Maybe it was his look which seemed to strip her down, made her entertain fantasies of a long, silk veil and a privately viewed belly dance—with an audience of only one.

A short breath escaped her, and Marie brought her palms to her cheeks which she knew were flaming red.

"Well, good," he said, looking deeply in her eyes. "Just as long as we're clear on that."

"Clear?" Marie asked, feeling as if she'd missed something.

"That the fit is right."

He smiled and all reason plummeted to her stocking-clad toes.

"You know, we offer an unconditional guarantee."

"I'll keep that in mind," she said, drawing her purse in at her side and turning quickly on her heels.

What was happening? Why in the world were her palms so sweaty and her legs trembling? Marie shot for the exit before her feet could give way.

She thanked him again for his help, then pushed her way out the door to the street. She breezed past the paper turkey hanging on the front glass wall of the eye doctor's office. Eye doctor, her foot. He was more like some kind of psychic. A seer who could look right through her... and into the deepest depths of her soul.

No, that was crazy! That sort of thing never happened. She'd only just laid eyes on him, for heaven's sake. So what if he had a body to die for, and a heart-stopping lopsided grin? So what if he'd asked her to lunch, indicating both his immediate interest and availability?

*She* was not available—that was the important part. Marie glanced down at the meager blue stone on her left hand that served as an engagement ring. One of these days, Cecil was going to save enough cash from serving lattes to buy her a *real* diamond... That would be shortly after he finally sold his book and hell froze over, she thought with a slow, sad smile.

She knew she should have more faith in Cecil, but, after five long years, it was getting hard. If only he weren't so faithful, it would have been a cinch to look for someone else. But the trouble with all those someone else's was that *she* wasn't good enough for them. Just like Paul, they'd nail her heart, then chase anything in a skirt.

Not Cecil. Good old, reliable, thirty-eight-year-old Cecil. Though he was only six years her senior, at times Marie swore he was pushing one hundred.

Marie found herself wondering briefly about the age of the optician. Though he was probably a little older than she, there was a vibrancy in his eyes that spoke of youthful vigor. Enduring vigor. A relentless, animalistic...

She stopped herself, shocked at where her mind was going. Right down to his form-fitting jeans and dockside loafers. Then back up again—past his rock-hard torso and unforgettable smile, to his unnerving, brilliant blue eyes.

No! She wouldn't do this! As she'd learned from her disastrous affair with Paul, animal attraction only went so far... before the other partner started monkeying around.

It was better this way. Better with Cecil. Though he might not be the most exciting man Marie had ever met, he was certainly the most dependable. Five years together and he hadn't cast a roving eye at a single other woman. They got along, had some laughs. And, even though he never could interest her in that deep-thinking literary fiction that always had him so enthralled, at least they both liked to read.

He worked in the cafe, she sold books. He, after all, wrote books—even if he couldn't sell them. There was a strange logic to their arrangement. And a comfort, too. From one day to the next, Marie knew that Cecil would be there. And until today... that had been enough.

David absentmindedly twirled his pencil, then tapped its eraser against his ledger. Someday soon, his boss Caroline was going to spend her profits wisely and hire an official accountant. In the meantime, David looked at his chance to serve as both optician and bookkeeper as an opportunity. Next year, when he planned to open his own shop, the financial experience would come in handy. Then, he sighed, any rules about employee-client fraternization would be self-imposed. Or, not.

David knew it was wrong, really wrong, to hit on the women who came in here. And he almost never did. But when they handed him their cell phone numbers with a wink and a smile and a maybe-we-can-see-each-other-sometime look, it was pretty damned hard to resist. He was a red-blooded male, just like the next guy. And when they had legs like Suzanne, or breasts like Rebecca....

David rubbed his temples and glared at the column of numbers in front of him, willing the insubordinate figures to make sense. But the only figure that stood out in his mind belonged to one Marie McCloud. Not that she was as voluptuous as some of the women he'd dated. Not even that she was more beautiful. But there was something in the way she'd widened her eyes when she'd looked at him. Something in the warm flush of color on her skin.

David shook his head, thinking himself stupid for believing they'd made any kind of meaningful connection.

He turned half-heartedly and scanned through the contacts on his cell phone. Thursday afternoon, already. If he hoped for a respectable date—or even a not-so-respectable one—by the weekend, David would have to start calling soon.

But suddenly, he had the unusual notion that he'd be more happy spending his Saturday night with a book.

Marie blew into the cafe like a gust of autumn wind and settled her purse on the counter.

"Decaf, darling?" Joanne smiled, swabbing a dollop of cream off the faux marble serving bar.

Marie stared back at the older woman, somehow unable to fix her gaze. "Yes. No. I mean, I don't—"

Joanne extended a wrinkled hand in Marie's direction. "Slow down there." She had to be in her seventies, but with her batik skirt and sleek silver braid, sometimes looked more like a willowy teenager gone prematurely gray.

Joanne dropped her rag and leaned forward with a conspiratorial whisper. "What's wrong, doll? That Cecil done some—"

She fell silent as the ponytailed man materialized at her side.

"Morning, Marie." He smiled, and his even teeth shone white beneath his aquiline nose.

Marie sighed. "It's way past noon, Cecil. How long have you been here?"

He swiveled his head and glared at the clock. "Oh, since nine. Time flies when you're having fun."

Marie groaned. "Short cappuccino, Joanne. Double foam, nix the caffeine."

"Hey, Marie," Cecil said, when Joanne went to steam the milk. "About our dinner tonight..."

Marie adjusted her new frames and fumbled for an excuse. Somehow, in light of her lunchtime encounter, eating with Cecil seemed downright unappetizing.

"I have some revisions to do."

Marie smiled as his meaning dawned.

"Oh, Cecil, of course I understand. I have a little project I'm working on myself." She drew a sharp breath, wondering where on earth that had come from.

"You do?" Cecil asked, his gray eyes narrowing. At one time Marie would have called the color smoldering, like embers. But right now it looked... like smog.

She pulled two singles from her wallet as Joanne set her coffee down in front of her, puzzling at her new perspective. Surely, twenty minutes with a handsome optician wouldn't—

"A book?" Cecil pressed.

"Has to be romance," Joanne chimed in, securing the lid on the paper cup.

But Marie just turned the color of a very ripe tomato, picked up her cappuccino and left.

This time of day, right before closing, Marie normally perused the aisles to be certain everything was shelved properly. The upscale store paid its staff well to ensure a user-friendly environment for the average book buyer. But occasionally there were slip-ups, like when a new employee mistakenly placed *Growing Old Gracefully* in with New Age category books.

Marie resisted the urge to linger in the paperback romance section. Her feet ached and her back was sore from all the bending and stooping involved in reviewing the day's new arrivals. She'd arranged two author signings and helped coordinate an event for the mystery book club that was originally scheduled to meet in the cafe, but got bumped by a big-name local musician who'd agreed to play there on Monday. A real coup for Books & Bistro, but a major headache for Marie, who needed to accommodate the sure-fire crowd that live music brought, while avoiding the ire of her hard-core mystery fans. They, after all, bought more books on a regular basis than any other group—apart from romance aficionados. As a compromise, she'd offered to help sponsor a "Who Done It" wine and cheese tasting in the store's lounge area, complete with samplings from "mystery" local vineyards whose identities would be revealed at the evening's end.

Marie blew a hard breath and sent a loose lock of hair flying. And to think she'd gotten into the bookstore business because she loved to read! She rarely ever had time for it. Which is why she was so often caught red-handed over her Danish and coffee with something just as steamy as her java.

She paused mid-stride, trying to remember which way she was going. Somehow her eye had fallen on one of those gloriously embossed crimson covers, the kind boasting a manly hero with an admirable show of muscle. The title said something about a pirate and his mistress. Marie studied the male model's tawny ponytail, comparing it to Cecil's. Well, he certainly had Cecil's hair, but the body definitely belonged to...

Marie snatched her glasses off her nose and humphed into the air. Twenty minutes. Twenty minutes was all he'd had. Yet somehow it had been enough to leave his mark. She'd felt as branded by his smile as by the hottest, deepest kiss. As ravaged by his eyes, as... Marie cleared her throat and placed her glasses back squarely where they belonged. She smiled pleasantly at a passing patron who nabbed the pirate book off the shelf and openly ogled its cover. Then blushed at the thought that she had probably looked just like that only hours ago—right in the center of the spectacle shop.

# Chapter Two

David made himself as comfortable as possible at the tiny cafe table. But no matter how he positioned his legs, his knees knocked against the low table top.

A ponytailed man wearing a forest green apron walked over, notepad in hand. "What will it be tonight?" he asked, his light eyes squinting.

David peered over the server's shoulders and into the book aisles. Well, he certainly couldn't order her. How much simpler life would be if you could just ask for what you really wanted. Marie McCloud, please. Single, with a dash of daring.

The waiter impatiently shuffled his feet.

"Coffee?" he asked, flipping his too-long ponytail over his shoulder.

If the man had to wear one, David decided, it would be much to his advantage to shear it an inch or two.

"Sure," David said, lowering his voice. "Say, you know any women in here?"

The waiter shot him a disgusted look.

Well, so maybe he wasn't into women. But, hey, he at least had to know who his coworkers were.

"Decaf or regular," the waiter deadpanned.

David read his name tag. "Look, Cecil."

Cecil raised one skeptical eyebrow.

"It's Cecil, right?"

"If you're in here to read, you're in the wrong section." He jutted his chin in the opposite direction. "Plenty of books over there."

David turned his head just in time to see the swish of a floral print skirt disappear behind the newsstand. His pulse shot up and his internal thermostat skyrocketed. The cold Virginia fall couldn't touch the current fire in his veins.

"I'll give you a minute to make up your mind," Cecil said, turning to go.

"No, wait!" David reached out a hand and the waiter recoiled. Not that it necessarily mattered to David. The only person he cared about right now stood about five foot six and had the smile of a vixen.

"Do you know that woman over there?"

Cecil raised an eyebrow. "You know, there's a ladies' night at the bar down the street..."

"Decaf is fine," David said, pushing back in his chair with a scowl.

What was this guy's problem? All David had done was ask one little innocent question. Okay, so maybe it was two.

Cecil returned quickly with a lukewarm cup of sludge that he passed off as coffee.

"Anything else?" he asked, setting down the ceramic mug.

Nothing, apparently, that this guy would help him with.

David studied the neat geometric patterns on the imitation tile floor, as Cecil tore a sheet from his pad and laid the check on the table.

"Listen..." Cecil surprised David by softening his businesslike tone. "Didn't mean to come off hard as nails earlier. It's been kind of a long day, if you know what I mean."

"Don't worry about it," David said, forcing a smile. Waiter-with-an-attitude probably wanted a tip.

Cecil pushed his pencil behind his ear in a professorial fashion and appeared to study his surly customer.

"Is it someone special? Or are you just in here shopping?"

David sighed and sipped from his cup. "I hate to shop."

"Ah, but you love to buy." Cecil folded his arms in front of him and looked smug when David didn't answer. "The direct approach always works well for me."

David gave Cecil's narrow shoulders a second look, wondering what he'd missed. A ladies' man? This guy? Well, he'd heard that some women liked the ultrasensitive, underfed type...

"Of course"—Cecil beamed—"it helps that women love artists."

"You're a painter?"

"Better yet. I write."

Better for this place, David guessed, casting a quick glance around the packed cafe. A few couples here and there. But mainly, plenty of women. Single women, David gauged, from what he knew of Covesville.

"So, then. You're into literary types, too?" David flashed Cecil his best let's-be-buds smile.

Cecil laughed. "Let's just say I've been around enough to know you can't always judge a book by its cover. And when you get between those covers..." He grinned. "You read me?" he asked with a wink. "These brainy girls"—his pale gray eyes scanned the room—"really dig a mind link. Give them an intellectual connection, and they're all yours."

"Mind link?"

"Sure, you know. Talk about Plato, or Voltaire. Meet them on their level."

The between the covers part, David understood, and Plato he'd heard of. But Voltaire sounded more like a fast car than an aphrodisiac. "So, it's books we're talking?"

"Of course, books." Cecil nabbed the bill off the table and scribbled some notes on its back. "Here are a few recommendations. And stick your nose in a *Publishers Weekly.* See what's hot."

"Cecil," David said, laying down a five-dollar tip, as Marie and an elderly woman walked by. "Thanks very much."

Marie leaned against the wall next to the water fountain in the narrow hallway and shook her head at Joanne.

"It's no use. I just can't pretend any longer."

"You're trying to tell me that all of this has happened in the last two days," Joanne said. "But my guess is, it's been building longer. I mean, look, I know you were disappointed with that puny excuse for an engagement ring."

Marie shoved her left hand deeper in the pocket of her nubby brown cardigan.

"He hasn't got it, Marie. Better you face it now than later. After, say, you've produced two or three kids together and are still waiting on that first advance check from a publisher."

"But what is *it,* Joanne? I've spent my whole life looking."

"Baby," Joanne said, patting her shoulder. "You weren't even born when I started my exploration of the great male species. The only thing I can tell you is when it's there, you know it. And when it ain't, no amount of wishful thinking will make it so."

Marie stayed still a moment, examining her friend. Though her ivory skin had wrinkled, there was an ageless quality to her features, an impish mischievousness in those coal-black eyes.

"Joanne, how is it that a hot mama like you never married?"

"Too busy being hot to cool down for the aisle, I suppose. Or maybe I just missed my chance and didn't know it."

Marie bit her lip and waited for her to finish.

"The thing is, Marie, my problem was always the opposite of yours."

"Opposite?"

"Yes, sweetie. Too into the physical aspect, that's what I was. Free love and all that. It came with the age. Age of Aquarius. I was an old maid of fifty then, and it was liberating!

"But for a spring chick like you..." Joanne clamped her hands around Marie's shoulders and stepped closer. "Honey, a nice girl like you deserves to have it all."

Marie tilted her chin toward the well-meaning older woman. "But I've had that. Don't you see? I've had all that hot-and-bothered stuff. And I ended up with a broken heart."

"And then you met Cecil, who's about as exciting as a dead fish. And you're finally starting to see that dead fish—like company—stink after three days." She grimaced. "Much less five years."

"Excuse me..."

Marie felt her skin go hot as a deep familiar voice rose over Joanne's shoulder.

"Could you ladies tell me where to find—"

Joanne stepped aside and there he was. A vision in trim white jeans and a navy sweatshirt that did nothing to conceal the raw power that lay beneath it.

"Well, what a surprise." He smiled and sent the whole room spiraling. "Marie, isn't it? Marie McCloud?" Oceans of blue crinkled slightly at their corners as the wave of his stare crashed over her.

"Umm, hmm," was all Marie could manage in the drowning silence.

Joanne whistled between her teeth and walked back into the store without saying a word.

"Friend of yours?" David asked, placing his hand up on the wall near Marie's head and inclining his body in her direction.

*Speak,* Marie willed herself. Say something. Anything. "You've got quite a memory for names, Mr.—"

"Actually, it's the faces I remember best," he said, dropping his chin a fraction lower. Not to mention that her body was one David couldn't forget. Somewhere beneath that fuzzy, wool sweater and modestly swishy skirt lay a very womanly form. He'd seen it at least a million times since Thursday. In his daydreams, that is.

"David," he offered with a smile. "The name is David. David Lake. The optician, remember?"

As if Marie could forget

"Although I don't think we were ever officially introduced."

She looked up at him with those big brown eyes and blinked. "Well, then, you had me at a disadvantage."

Not as much as he would have liked.

A fine wash of color was working its way across her face, but she stood her ground—burgundy suede boots planted firmly in place, daring him with her damnably intoxicating eyes.

"Sorry about that," he said. "Not many clients are really all that interested in knowing my name."

"I doubt that," she said, stunned at where that courage had come from. Flirting! She was *flirting* with the most godlike male she'd laid eyes on in a decade and her fiancé was right in the next room!

"Excuse me..." said another familiar voice.

Marie swung her head around and choked. "Cecil!" she said, coughing past the lump in her throat.

"Jeez, Marie," he said, leaning forward and giving her arm a little squeeze. "Just going to the stock room. You look like you've seen a ghost!"

He gave David a curious glance. "You be sure she gives you good service, now! If there's anyone here who can get you what you want, it's Marie." Then he slipped between them and headed for the back of the store.

Marie didn't worry about blushing in front of David anymore. She was sure, by now, that he assumed crimson was her natural color.

In light of what had just transpired, David seemed remarkably nonchalant. He just propped his hand back up on the wall in its pre-warmed spot and smiled sweetly.

"Is he always that friendly?" David asked.

No, she'd been wrong. His hand wasn't propped exactly where it had been before. It was higher now. Off center. In a way that enabled him to stand even closer than the first time. Close enough to leave Marie completely overcome by his delectable aroma. The manly scent that would intoxicate her, if he'd only stay near.

"Pardon?" she asked. Knowing, just knowing, that whatever he'd said had flown right past her. Boy, this was bad. Badder than bad. She had to find a way out of here so she could think!

"Cecil."

"Cecil? You know him?"

A rich, bubbling laughter erupted from his chest. "No, not really." David paused and cocked one eyebrow. "But he sure seemed to know you. Boyfriend?"

"No," Marie said, biting her bottom lip. "I mean, friends, yeah, sure. Good ol' Cecil is friends with the world!" Never once in the past five years had she lied about her relationship with Cecil. But since those feelings were now so unclear, was it really lying at this point?

"Yeah, I know his type," David said in a conspiratorial whisper. "Regular Don Juan."

"What?" Marie ducked her head and inched back a step so David no longer held her prisoner.

David dropped his arm to his side. She'd gone from embarrassed red to positively white. "Did I say something to upset you?"

"No. Not at all." Marie felt the heat well within her like an exploding volcano. "It's just that Cecil..." She gave a noncommittal laugh.

"Oh, I know," David said, his eyes wide with amazement. "Not what you'd expect at all. But I guess it's romantic to look like a starving artist. I've heard some people find that very exciting."

"Well, I guess some—"

"Like you, for instance?"

"Me? Oh, heavens..." Marie stammered. "Well, you know, I don't think I could really say."

"But he is popular with the—literary types, I mean."

Marie wrinkled up her nose. Hey, wait a minute. Wait just one minute! All this talk about *Cecil?* Oh my God, David wasn't... couldn't possibly be asking because...

"What," he asked, with utmost innocence. "What in the world are you staring at? Did I get coffee on my sweatshirt or something?"

"Are you interested in Cecil?"

David just looked at her for a long moment. A slow grin spread across his face. "Me? Holy cow, *me?*" He sputtered and began to laugh.

Marie gripped her own face in horror, realizing her terrible mistake.

"I only just met him today. Besides," he said, with a teasing grin, "he's not my type."

Marie arched both eyebrows above her turquoise wire frames.

"Females, Marie. I like females," he said, emphasizing the word by making a curving gesture with his two sturdy hands.

"Oh," she said, exhaling slowly. "I'm sorry. So sorry if I implied—"

"Well, there's a first time for everything, I suppose. Not that I'd ever—*ever* been accused of..."

She looked positively petrified.

"It was a misunderstanding," David said, steadying her shoulders in his strong grip. "Really. Let's forget all about it."

A jolt of sensation ripped through her and she felt somehow awakened by his touch, all over her body.

"Hey," he said, brushing the back of his hand over her burning cheek. "All's forgiven. Really."

Forgiven, maybe. Forgotten, never. Marie had the feeling she'd always remember this. No matter what, she couldn't erase the memory of his tender touch, of an attraction so real, so physical that Marie's only punishment would be in his letting go.

But this was wrong. Terribly, terribly wrong. Despite the way he looked at her, despite the way he made her feel, she'd made her pledge to another man.

"David," Marie said, her breath catching in her throat. "I'm engaged."

David blanched and crammed his hands into his jeans pockets.

"Engaged! Well, isn't that terrific! Ah, what a great coincidence that is."

"It is?" Marie asked, the blood draining from her face.

"Why, sure. You're the bookstore manager, aren't you?"

Marie nodded.

"Then who better to help me pick out a wedding planner?"

"Wedding planner? *You're* engaged?"

He gave her a humble smile that sent shivers down her—very committed, she reminded herself—spine. "Not me, my sister."

Well, it was a half truth, David told himself. Debbie had already been engaged three times. The fourth time was sure to follow.

Marie was embarrassed at the rush of relief that came at his words. The image that immediately came to mind of David Lake looking handsome in a tuxedo and a boutonniere was enough to make her hear wedding bells.

"So, you'll help?" he asked, his blue eyes shining.

Marie swallowed hard and directed him to the entertainment and weddings section, her knees trembling ever so slightly with each new step. Really, she thought, giving herself a swift mental kick, the last thing you should have read during your dinner break was the wedding scene from *Groom To Be.*

When Marie got home later that evening, she was surprised to find a note from Cecil taped to her computer.

*Great news,* it said, *finally got that check from Knopf...*

Knopf? Cecil had sold a book to Alfred A. Knopf? If he'd already gotten the advance money, it had to have been weeks ago.

*Diane and I...*

Diane? The cappuccino girl with the body piercings?

Oh, God. Marie plopped down in her chair and tugged off her boots.

She yanked off her glasses, polished them with a tissue, then set them back on her nose, remembering something. Cecil and the lithe twenty-two-year-old Diane huddled over a back issue of *Publishers Weekly* sharing some private joke.

Yep. It was Diane, all right.

*Diane and I have moved to New York. Please try to understand and please don't call. I'll come back for my stuff in a few months if you'd like to box it up.*

*Cecil.*

## Chapter Three

David held the big wedding planner in his hands and flipped through its spiral-bound pages.

"You getting hitched?" Caroline asked, her voice weighted with skepticism.

David spun in his chair to face his blond bombshell boss. Funny how he'd stopped noticing how good-looking she was the moment she'd started barking out orders. She was a tough businesswoman, but fair. And, not so incidentally, a contented wife and the mother of two children. Definitely off limits. Caroline chided him about settling down, in a tolerant big-sisterly way. Not that she was that much older, but her superior professional status brought out the mother hen in her. David suspected he was about to get pecked on.

"Can't a man do a little leisure reading on his lunch hour?" David asked, with mock defensiveness.

"Sure, read these," she said, dropping a stack of files on his desk.

David leaned back in his chair and propped his feet up on his desk, crossing his legs comfortably at the ankles.

"You can work me like a slave driver eight hours a day, but these forty-five minutes," he said, clutching the thick planner to his chest, "are mine!"

"All right, big boy," she said, laying a hand on her hip. "What's in there? Honeymoon lingerie, perhaps?" She made a move toward the book.

"Not so fast," David said, holding her back with an extended hand.

"It's not..." Caroline's slender shoulders sagged. "Tell me it's not your sister Debbie heading down the aisle yet again."

"It's not Debbie," he said with a flawless grin.

"Okay, David," Caroline said with a giant lunge in his direction, "give it here."

She caught one end of the large book in her hand and tugged.

"Hey!" he yelped, dropping his feet to the floor, as a sheaf of papers spilled forth. "Give that back!"

"David, I swear, if there's something pornographic in—"

Caroline yanked and the planner tumbled to the floor, pages fanning out in wild disarray.

"What's this?" she asked, nabbing an unfolded brochure off the floor. "A Books & Bistro events calendar?"

"Oh my God, David," she said, furiously fanning her face with the flyer. "This is worse than I thought! You're actually reading!"

Marie crumpled up another tear-stained tissue and added it to the heap on the floor. In the three years since she'd been promoted to manager, she could count the times she'd called in sick on one hand. And today was one of them.

Cecil and Diane? How could she have been so blind? And right under her nose!

And what—if anything—did the mysterious heartthrob David Lake know about all this? *A regular Don Juan,* he'd said in reference to Cecil. Marie clutched her stomach, fearing she would throw up. How many? Just how many

other women had there been, then? Five? Fifteen, twenty?
Oh, God.

Marie stood and rushed to the bathroom where she
vomited violently.

Thank God she wasn't pregnant, she thought, as her
bare knees hit the cold tile floor. She rested her head in her
hands over the porcelain john, recalling Cecil's recent
suggestion that they make a baby.

"Don't you think it'd be better if we got married first?"
was all she had asked.

He'd stormed out the door, and not come back for five
hours—at which time he'd produced a bouquet of limp
daisies and a half-hearted apology. "One commitment at a
time," was what he'd said.

It had been a cruel thing to say, knowing how badly
Marie wanted a child. For a while, she thought she'd never
want to have her own. But, as time moved on and that old
biological clock started ticking, she'd begun to change her
mind.

After her parents' car accident, she'd practically raised
her four younger brothers and sisters. Her mother had died
instantly, and her father had become permanently disabled.
At age sixteen, Marie had been thrust into the role of
running the household, scrounging together nutritious
meals on the meager checks from her dad's disability
payments.

Those had been some dreadful days. Coming of age as
a woman and yearning for her mother, all the while having
to hide that fact because "mother" was precisely what she
had to be.

Marie stood and splashed cold water on her face,
feeling better.

Now, each of her siblings was on his own. Her two sisters married, Johnny engaged, and Mark just enrolled in graduate school. She'd done a good job with them, she supposed. But then again, so had her father. He'd been a rock for the family until he'd died last spring. Always keeping his chin up, despite his paralysis. Never too tired or preoccupied to listen.

Marie knew her sometimes unruly brothers wouldn't have turned out nearly as well without their father's patient wisdom to guide them. At times, they'd driven Marie so crazy with their teenage antics, that her only refuge had been to escape to her room with a book.

Reading had seen her through the difficult times. No matter what was going on outside her bedroom door, she could curl up under the covers and imagine that someday a handsome prince would come along to take her away from all of it.

But all the handsome princes in Marie's high school class went off to college while she had to stay home and help support the family.

Her first job in a bookstore was heaven. She felt a comfort in the unending rows of books, a special camaraderie with the host of unexplored fictional characters—just waiting for her touch to reveal their secret worlds.

Marie walked to the kitchen and poured herself a glass of water, wondering what she would do with herself today. It had been at least a year since she'd had a Sunday off. She was out of books and out of money, and the local library was closed. Oh well, she thought, flipping on the coffeemaker. There was always a walk in the park. Maybe the fresh air would do her good.

David pulled back as Jupiter strained at the leash.

"Whoa there, boy! Hang on!"

But it was David who was hanging on for dear life as the black Lab fixated on the squirrel with a whine, and then another... *yank!*

David stumbled forward as the big dog broke free and bolted into the trees.

He rubbed his sweaty palms on his pants and looked frantically in all directions. Now what was he going to do? Caroline would kill him if he lost her stupid dog.

"Jupiter! Here, fella!" he called in his biggest, booming voice.

Nothing.

He forcefully clapped his hands together and tried again.

There was a slight rustling in the bushes behind the park fountain.

"Jupiter!"

The movement stopped.

David had an idea. He placed two fingers between his teeth, spun around and whistled—hard.

"Most people just say hello."

David jerked his head sideways.

There stood Marie McCloud in a knee-length overcoat, hands fitted tightly over both ears. Her cheeks were flushed with morning cold, her lips the prettiest shade of pink.

For a moment David forgot all about the dog.

"Marie!"

"What," she asked, giving the park a suspicious sweep of her eyes, "exactly are you doing?"

"Oh," he said, letting out a full breath that clouded the air, "looking for Jupiter."

Marie's eyebrows shot up. "Hate to tell you this, but I think you'd have better luck at night."

David looked blank. Blank, but incredibly handsome, she decided. Even in his ratty gray sweats, and sky-blue parka. Didn't hurt that the color of his coat matched his gorgeous eyes.

"Oh!" he smiled, his whole face lighting up. Then he laughed in that rich, rumbling baritone Marie liked so much.

"Not the planet," he said patiently. "Jupiter is Caroline's dog."

Oh, Marie thought, as disappointment hit her hard. So he *was* taken. She felt her temper begin to simmer. Taken, and yet he'd still invited her to lunch?

Marie stared down at the leash dangling in David's hand. "Well, I'm sure Caroline won't be any more upset about you losing her dog than you hitting on your clientele."

"Client..." David's voice fell off, as his face turned a hue akin to purple.

"One question, David," Marie asked, her anger growing. "Do you always make passes at girls who wear glasses? Or, was I special?"

"I, uh..."

His neck was crimson, and his ears so vivid they looked like they were about to fall off.

At that moment, a frisky black Lab bounded out of the bushes and made a beeline for her knees.

"Hey there, big guy," she said, bending to scratch the salivating animal behind its ears.

Marie stuck out a hand and snatched the leash, instantly clamping it on to Jupiter's collar in one deft move.

"Go home to Caroline, David," she said, standing and handing over the lead.

"Home?"

Marie turned and began walking out of the park.

"Wait!" David said, racing to meet her, Jupiter galloping at his side. "Caroline's not at home!"

Marie cast him a sideways glance through heir glasses. "Sorry, David. I'm not into that. You'll have to do your two-timing with someone else."

She picked up her pace and kept going.

"No, you don't under—"

Jupiter collapsed in a heap and rolled sideways.

"Get up!" David pulled on the leash, but Jupiter just lowered his head to the pavement, tongue lolling out.

David looked up at Marie's curvy figure disappearing through the morning fog.

"Wait! Don't go! You've got it all..."

But it was too late. She'd already melted into the mist.


David put down the book and rubbed his temples. Holy cow, this was going to be even harder than he thought. What was the deal with this stuff, anyway? The dialogue wasn't even in quotation marks, for God's sake. So how in heaven's name was he supposed to know who was saying what? Much less thinking it?

David massaged his aching knees in frustration and stood to grab a beer.

He walked to the refrigerator, picked up a bottle and popped the top. Was she really worth it? David had never done anything like this before. Gone completely overboard for some woman. Some women who was *engaged,* for crying out loud. And she disapproved of him anyway, because she thought he had a woman named Caroline at home.

Marie was neatly tied up in a relationship that meant matrimony eventually. But then again, maybe it didn't. That was the hope David clung to. He knew from his sister Debbie's experiences that engaged women didn't necessarily walk down the aisle every time. Heck, for some women, it seemed to be a whole lot like shopping. Don't like the man after a while, return him. Nonetheless, David wanted to believe that once Marie committed to him, her shopping around would be over.

David froze as an ice-cold swig sliced down his throat.

Of course, that meant that his shopping around would be over as well... No more late nights with Candy, the aerobics instructor, or Lizbeth, his sexy new mechanic.

David took another swig of beer, letting the panic pass.

He was getting way ahead of himself here. Thinking about happily-ever-after! Holy cow. That wasn't what he wanted...

Was it?

He wanted Marie's attention, sure. But the exasperating woman didn't seem to want to give him a second look.

At first, there'd been a gleam in her eyes. That telling sparkle that told David he had half a chance...

But after the park, she'd acted like she could barely stand the sight of him. Even when he went into her store to buy some of Cecil's recommendations.

He'd approached her directly, but she'd claimed she was busy setting up some kind of wine tasting and assigned a flunky to help him.

Give him a break! Did Marie really expect David to believe they'd be serving wine in a bookstore? They couldn't possibly have a liquor license. Unless, of course, the brother of the guy who owned the place, who just happened to be the sheriff, had called in some favors at City Hall.

David set his beer on the counter, and began to imagine himself and Marie running down the steps of City Hall, hand in hand, smiling and happy. Her dark, wavy hair was piled high and studded with wildflowers, sweet curls breaking free to frame her glowing face.

David coughed loudly and shook his head. Next he would be seeing babies!

Better get back to his reading, he thought, carrying his brew to the armchair. All this fantasizing was getting him nowhere. And David Lake wasn't made for dreams. He was built for action.

Now, if he could just finish this blasted book, then maybe he'd be able to convince Marie his actions spoke louder than words.

# Chapter Four

Marie surrendered the floor to a round of applause.

"Thanks, Chad," she said, walking over and taking the sheriff's hand.

"No problem, hon." He smiled as his silver hair caught the light. "I like a good who-done-it just as much as the next guy." He leaned forward and winked. "Just as long as the bad guy winds up behind bars."

"Didn't know you had the time for reading, Sheriff."

Chad let out a laugh. "Well, I'll tell you a secret if you keep it quiet..." He brought his head to hers and whispered in her ear, "The life of crime is dead in Covesville."

Marie laughed and patted Chad on the arm. "Since you've got to be here anyway, pull up a chair and join us."

"Think I'll do that," Chad said. "To tell you the truth, Marie, it's been kind of hard to fill the hours since my Emily passed away."

She caught a glimpse of Joanne, bending low to shelve books at the far end of the aisle.

"I know it's been a rough couple of years," she said, smiling warmly at the older gentlemen. "You sit. Plenty here to take your mind off that extra time you've got on your hands."

Then she walked down the aisle and asked Joanne to take Chad a complimentary glass of Chablis.

"Mind if I join you?"

Marie raised her eyes from *Destiny's Desire* just in time to see David break into a broad grin.

"Looks good," he said, surveying the flesh-revealing cover.

She settled her book next to her cup of cold coffee and checked her watch. "Not working today?"

"Boss gave me the day off."

"Look, David," Marie said, stopping him from pulling out a chair, "I'm really not interested."

"Of course, it helped that I took such good care of her dog."

He must have showered just for the occasion and put on an extra splash of cologne, because he smelled even sexier than the last time he'd been this close. The time he'd laid his strong, masculine hands on her yielding flesh...

Wait a minute! That was *Destiny* talking. Destiny, the heroine from her steamy historical novel who had the hots for a man named Cane. A man she'd sworn was sweeter than sugar.

David picked another chair at the table and sat down, undaunted.

"Hey, that Jupiter was a real handful."

"Jupiter?" she asked, stifling her surprise.

"Sure, you've met him. Big, black hairy beast with a penchant for civil disobedience."

If she'd been outdoors, Marie was certain her glasses would have fogged with embarrassment.

"Are you telling me that Jupiter, the dog you were with, belongs to your boss—Caroline?"

David nodded. "Caroline Richards, a real taskmaster."

"So why take care of her dog?"

"Oh, well, she needed a favor. Besides," he said, leaning over with a whisper, "I have a soft spot for the physically challenged."

"Oh, poor woman," Marie said, thinking of her father. "What's she got?"

"Two kids and a husband," David answered.

"What's so challenging..." Marie thought of her brothers and stopped herself. "Was that supposed to be funny?" she asked David, who had begun toying with her book.

She slapped her hand down hard upon its cover to prevent him from picking it up.

David coolly withdrew his hand and settled it under his square jaw. He gazed into her eyes, seeming to search for something.

She was even more gorgeous than he remembered. Tastefully dressed in a black turtleneck sweater that made the most of her curves. If only he could figure a way to get her fiancé out of the way... Out of the way of those beautiful brown eyes.

"Has anyone ever told you how pretty you are?"

Marie stood abruptly from her chair, knocking the tabletop with her knees and sending her coffee dregs sloshing.

David sprung to his feet and piled napkins on the mess.

"Whoa! Hey! Where are you going?"

"Coffee break's over, David. My boss didn't give me the day off."

Unbelievable, Marie thought, leaving him there with coffee dribbling on his shoes. Utterly unbelievable!

"Well, I really don't see what the harm was in a cup of coffee," Joanne said, as she closed down her register.

"It wasn't the coffee, Joanne, but the sugar that went with it."

Joanne smiled understandingly and shook out her hair. It wasn't often she wore it that way, long and straight down her back, salt and pepper streaks enlivening the gray.

"I think he's sweet on you."

Marie scanned the day's receipts, then set down her clipboard. If she didn't know better, she'd swear Joanne was humming a love song.

"Jo-anne?"

Joanne looked over with a distant smile.

"Something going on I should know about?"

"As my boss or my friend?" Joanne asked.

Marie tapped her fingers against her chin. "Why, Joanne Bright, to look at you one would almost think there was a man in your life!"

Joanne turned the most curious shade of peachy-amber.

"No need to sound so surprised, love. You're the one who turned him on to me."

"Chad?" Marie asked, trying to keep her jaw from dropping.

Sure, that had been her idea. But she'd never dreamed it would work. Chad and his late wife Emily had been together since grade school. He'd never in his life looked at another woman.

"What?" Joanne asked, setting both hands on her hips. "Did you think me incapable?"

Oh, no, Marie definitely believed Joanne was capable.

Marie felt her lips pull apart in a half laugh, half smile.

"Oh, Joanne," she said, rushing forward and taking her friend in her arms. "I'm so happy for you."

"Thanks, sweetie," Joanne said, returning the hug and patting Marie soundly on the back. "Now, it's your turn."

Marie pulled back, suddenly overcome with emotion.

"Oh," she said, tears spilling forth, "Joanne."

"Hey, hey," Joanne said, stepping forward and taking Marie in her arms again. "Everything's going to be all right."

Marie shook her head, her eyes hot, her lips trembling—grateful that, at this hour, no one else was left in the store.

"You just don't understand, Jo. I've had my chances. Two of them. And I blew them both."

"You, angel, didn't blow anything. It was those devils disguised as men who did the damage."

"They're all devils," Marie said, more tears bursting forth. "Demons... with the impulse to destroy."

"Well, maybe he's not like that."

Marie lifted her head from Joanne's shoulder and stared into her eyes with a betrayed look.

"He thinks I'm engaged, Joanne. *Engaged.* And today he had the audacity to call me pretty."

Joanne gasped and brought her free hand to her mouth. "The gall!"

Marie softened her anguished face into a semblance of a smile.

"Sweetheart," Joanne said, dabbing Marie's damp cheek with a tissue. "You shouldn't blame the poor man for being persistent. You are quite a catch, after all."

"Joanne," Marie said, holding the older woman so tightly she nearly breathed her in, "you should have been a mother."

"Well, to see that old coot Chad in action," Joanne said, with a shy grin, "I would almost swear he's working on it."

David scanned the groom's checklist for maybe the twelfth time in the last two hours. He closed the wedding planner wearily.

"Ridiculous," he said, sighing out loud. If all the to-dos on that list were optical prescriptions to be filled, David would be grinding glass indefinitely.

And, from what David had heard, that would only be the start of it. After the wedding, then the honey-dos would begin. "Honey, do this..." and "Honey, do that."

David caught himself smiling and realized with surprise that he'd actually enjoy Marie ordering him around. He stretched back in his chair indulging in a fantasy about just what she might order him to do. But his fun was interrupted by his ringing cell.

"David, this is Caroline. Look, I have to wait at the doctor's office with Sally. Hope you can hold down the fort the rest of the afternoon."

David swung his feet to the floor and cleared his throat.

"Sure thing, Caroline. Been working like a madman, but another hour or two alone won't kill me."

"Thanks, David, I really owe you."

"No problem, boss. Say, how is your little girl anyway? That fever of hers any better?"

"Not really." Caroline huffed into the phone. "The nurse thinks she might have chicken pox."

"Chicken pox? Holy cow."

"Yeah, right, say a prayer. Please. I can't have chicken pox right now. The nurse says she'll have to stay out of daycare for at least two weeks. I knew I should have gotten her that vaccine, but Jim insisted..." Her voice dropped off and David could tell she was covering her cell while she talked to someone else. "...Oh. Oh, okay, just another minute," she was saying.

"David? You still there?"

David slid the wedding planner in his desk drawer and shut it.

"You bet. Hey, I'm awfully sorry about Sally."

"You and me both! Well, anyway, the receptionist says I have to get off the phone. I really appreciate your filling in."

"This afternoon's no problem, Caroline. Don't you worry."

"This afternoon? David, I'm talking about possibly the next two weeks."

Two weeks with no supervision and the whole place to himself? David grinned wickedly, because he knew she couldn't see it.

"You can count on me to keep things humming."


Marie stretched out her neck and rolled her head on her shoulders. She'd been having trouble getting into the swing of things all day, and now this. Her children's storyteller called in sick. Something about a chicken pox epidemic, and guess whose kids had it?

She shrugged and tried to work out the tension in her shoulders but it was useless. In less than twenty minutes, she'd have to put on her most sunshiny face and go greet the mini-masses.

Oh well, she thought, studying the shelves for something appropriate, that's what being a manager meant. When someone didn't show, you stepped in. The show must go on, and all that. Particularly with the sales the children's department had been racking up since Marie had initiated story hour.

Marie sat on the cushioned stool and watched as the kids filed in, grown-ups in tow. Mothers, mostly. But there were one or two dads. And, oh yes, how sweet—a set of grandparents.

"Well, boys and girls," she began, after checking the wall clock. "Does anybody know what month this is?"

"Novemberary!" somebody shouted.

Marie smiled warmly at the little boy in oversized britches. "Very good... You're Tommy, right?"

Tommy ran a hand through his curly red hair and beamed from ear to ear.

She'd thought she'd recognized him from last week when he'd come by to search for birthday books with his mother.

"Right! November! And who here in this very intelligent crowd can tell me what holiday comes in November?"

David followed the turkey noises to the back of the store. The older lady at the front desk—-Joanne, he thought, she said her name was—told him that Marie was doing story hour. David hadn't been exactly sure what that meant until he came upon Marie and the group of children following her.

David half hid himself behind a cardboard book display and watched in amazement as Marie led a line of unruly "turkeys" around the children's book department. Amazingly, it looked like even a couple of grandparents had joined in!

Marie stopped and pulled the glasses off her nose, laughing as a giggling band of children thrust themselves at her legs. She was enchanting, David realized. Absolutely charming...

And, he remembered, as someone rudely nudged past him, engaged to someone else.

David was just regaining his balance, when a second person pushed by him, completely upsetting his footing. David cast one desperate glance in Marie's direction and saw her meet his eyes with a horrified look, as he grabbed the softcover book display and carried it with him as he crashed to the floor.

For what seemed like endless seconds, David kept his nose buried in a mound of tumbled paperbacks, praying he'd awaken from this nightmare.

And then he felt her hand on his shoulder.

"David?"

It was Marie's voice. Marie's beautiful, soft voice. David swallowed hard and looked up.

"Oh my God, David! What happened? Are you okay?"

Well, at least he didn't look damaged. Only embarrassed, as well he should be. Pulling her latest merchandise to the floor. Really. What was it about this man that was just so...

Hunky, Marie thought, as he brought himself up on all fours and stared into her eyes. Heavens, he looked like a panther in that pose. And his smell...

Marie's eyes flashed at the suggestion, but then she shut them tight, recalling where she was.

"Here," she said, extending a hand, "let me help you up."

"Marie," he said, dusting off his jeans. "I'm so sorry. I'll pay for the damage. And help pick up. Whatever you want me to do."

She tried not to let herself think too hard about that, and picked up a couple of books to examine their spines.

"I think they'll live," she said, trying to sound flip while struggling to control the butterflies in her stomach.

"I ruined your story hour," David said, his face sagging as scattered hordes of children made their departure.

Marie tugged at the neck of her dress that suddenly seemed too tight.

"Oh, no. Really. Story hour was just winding down."

David righted the cardboard display and started restocking it with books, his muscular buttocks tensing under denim with each swinging movement of his arm.

Marie found herself unwilling to leave him there all alone, what with the buxom brunette in the corner who seemed to be making the same study of David's anatomy.

"Say," she said, once he had neatly finished up. "You're pretty good at that. Need a job?"

"I'm not unemployed, if that's what you're thinking."

"No, but..." It was hard to keep the smile from creeping onto her lips.

"What? What is it?" David gave himself a quick once-over, as if to verify that his clothes weren't on backwards.

"I was just thinking," Marie said, "that you must be doing a doggone good job with Jupiter for Caroline to give you all this time off."

David gave her a disarming smile that made Marie wish she hadn't started this banter.

Slow down, girl, she told herself, drowning in his deep blue eyes. You 're getting in way over your head.

"She's given me the rest of the afternoon," David said, diving into her with his stare. "Got plans?"

Marie wanted to say yes, prepared to tell him to go take a long walk off a short pier.

But then he crinkled his eyes and his playful lips turned up in another uneven smile, and she told him she left work at six o'clock.

## Chapter Five

"Where are we going?" Marie asked, as David held open the door to Books & Bistro, letting her leave first. He had a bulging green backpack slung over his shoulder and was wearing the same blue parka she remembered from the park.

"It's a surprise," he said, with a mischievous smile.

Marie wasn't so sure she should be setting herself up for surprises with this man. He'd already surprised, her enough, with the way he sent her pulse racing, and her emotions all out of kilter.

She scanned the small gravel parking area. Inside the ultra posh Books & Bistro, Marie could almost envision herself being in any cosmopolitan city in the world. But once she stepped out into the fading Virginia twilight and caught a glimpse of the Blue Ridge Mountains, she knew she was very much at home.

Covesville wasn't really much to speak of. There was this strip mall and a few downtown restaurants, plus a park, the mountain lake, and the small but distinguished women's college that sat high on a hill in the center of town.

"Where's your car?" she asked, noticing he had stopped on the curb.

"No car," he said, bending to open a padlock attached to a chain wound round a brick pillar and through the back wheel of a glistening ten-speed bicycle. "We're going by bike."

Marie gasped and brought her hands to her cheeks, staring down at her short cashmere dress.

"Don't worry," he said, throwing her a wink. "You'll be riding on back. I won't see a thing."

"Say," he said, shooting a glance at the bookstore. "Isn't there someone you need to call?"

"Call?" Marie asked, still wondering how she was going to modestly lift her leg over the high bar of that man's bicycle.

" Fiancé, maybe?" David said, feeling he had to ask.

Okay, he told himself, let's get this all out in the open. Acknowledge what you know. Woo her in a gentlemanly fashion. Then, after she's had a glass of wine—or two—ask her how serious she is about this guy, anyway.

"No," Marie said, giving a little cough. "No one to call.

"Now," she asked, buttoning up her lambs wool coat. "How do I mount this thing?"

David took a deep breath and strapped his backpack to a rack above the rear wheel. He wasn't altogether sure he'd be able to pedal straight with her riding his seat, her cushiony bosom pressed up against his back...

He felt his ears go tingly and knew he was reddening from the neck up.

"Here," he said, swinging his leg over the bike, "let me get on first, then I'll help you."

David steadied himself above the bar, then turned to look at her.

"Just hang on to my shoulders and hop on. The seat's all yours. I'll ride standing."

"Standing?" Marie asked, settling her rump on the hard leather seat and doing her best to tug down her creeping hemline. "Then how will I—"

But her words were lost in a rush of wind, as David lifted his lean hips and started to pedal.

David picked up speed and wheeled out of the parking lot, heading north.

Marie found herself clinging on for dear life to—of all things—David's rear end. She tried to center her hands on his undulating hips, but they kept slipping forward as he increased his movement with the speed of the bike. Oh my, she thought as the fingers of her right hand cupped around something hard in his jeans pocket.

She jerked her hands up to his waistline, but the bike wheels met the stones of an old dirt road and her left hand mistakenly traveled down his rock-hard thigh.

"Marie, sweetheart"—David grinned as he peered over his shoulder—"maybe we should wait until we get where we're going."

Her face burned as hot as three-alarm chili. Oh my God, he thought she was attacking him!

"Where are we going?" she yelled above the cross-winds.

Marie slipped her hands under his parka and grabbed for the waistband of his jeans, digging her thumbs under his leather belt. There, she thought, gripping his hips with splayed fingers. Now everything would stay put.

Well, well, David thought, grinning to himself. He was enjoying this ride even more than he thought he would. He'd been right about Marie. Right from the start. They had chemistry together, her fiancé be damned.

He shifted gears and brought the bike to a moderate crawl.

"Almost there," he told her, wondering why she had stopped doing what she'd been doing. Well, there'd be plenty of time for that. Plenty of time to allow those lovely fingers to explore.

David steered his bike into a clearing by a group of pines. Ahead of them, the quiet waters of Grassy Creek glimmered in the fading light, catching a purplish reflection of the distant mountains.

"A picnic?" Marie asked, as David dismounted and helped her get off the bike. Despite the fact that she'd lived here all her life, places like this were breathtaking still.

The breeze picked up and Marie huddled her arms around herself for warmth.

"Too chilly for you?" David asked, heating her with his smile.

"No, I'll be all right," she said, poking at the backpack he was carrying. "What's cooking?"

"Well," he said, looking around, then settling on a spot not too far from the water."How do submarine sandwiches and wine sound?"

Marie heaved a sigh, grateful he hadn't decided on one of those fat-free tofu dinners Cecil had been so fond of.

"Perfect," she said, grabbing one end of the red plaid blanket and helping David stretch it flat on the ground. Maybe, just maybe, this would go well.

"Marie," David said, uncorking the bottle as she decided where to put the knees that insisted on sneaking out of her too-short-for-a-picnic length dress. "I hope you're not getting the wrong impression from all of this."

She blinked hard, thinking she couldn't have heard him correctly. This was a date, right? A romantic waterside picnic by Grassy Creek.

David placed two plastic cups on the blanket and filled each halfway before looking up. "I mean, I know you're committed to someone else and I'd never—"

"Never what, David? Ask out a woman who was engaged? Pursue her relentlessly in her place of business? Fall all over the floor of her store?"

David hoped that the elongating shadows from the pines hid his slight frown. She was supposed to be impressed by his gentlemanly reserve. Not, as was apparent, ticked off.

"I couldn't help myself," he said, handing her some wine, then holding his own in her direction.

She accepted the cup and took a long swallow without making a toast.

"Marie, you've got to listen to me," he said, desperate for the words that would bring her back to bicycle mode. "I'm not the cad you think I am. I'm a gentleman, really."

She arched both eyebrows over her turquoise wire frames and downed another sip of wine before speaking.

"Well, well," she said, her eyes showing a dangerous amount of emotion. "Prove it."

Uh-oh, this was a trap and David knew it. "Ah sure, anything. What can I do?"

"It's what you can say, David."

A trick! He knew it. Holy cow. David held his breath and counted to ten, before exhaling slowly. "All right then, so what is it you want me to say?"

Marie put down her wine and stared out at the sun that was sinking below the shadowy mountains. "What I'd like, what I'd really like, is for you to give me something no other man has."

David sat at attention, liking the sound of this.

"The truth."

It was David's turn to drink some wine. And he did, emptying his entire cup. "Okay," he began cautiously. "I'll give you the truth. What kind of truth are you looking for?"

Marie turned her deep brown eyes upon his and David could've sworn he was falling off a cliff.

"I've got to know why, David. Why me? Or is it just me—and not a whole slew of others?"

David shifted his position just slightly, feeling cornered. Of course, it was just her! She'd tortured him, turned him inside out. He'd been so far gone he was actually reading wedding planners and literary fiction, for crying out loud! Still, David couldn't deny the feminine names that took up so much space on his contact list any more than he could ignore the pounding in his chest.

"Nobody's ever done for me what you do," he said, settling on a truth that wouldn't give too much away.

"Ah, but," she said, shaking a scolding finger in his direction, "are there others out there still doing it for you?"

That seemed like a mighty personal question from a woman who was supposedly engaged.

"And what if there were?" David asked. "What precisely would it be to you?"

"Nothing," she said, her face expressionless in the near darkness.

"Nothing?" he asked, riveted to his soul.

Marie was startled by the pain she saw in his eyes. He'd wanted her to care. Wanted her to say she hoped he'd be her one and only, with eyes for no one else.

David pulled a couple of submarine sandwiches from his backpack.

"Might as well eat," he said, handing her a paper package. "Never good to drink on an empty stomach."

Marie had to agree. The one cup of wine she'd had was going to her head. She felt dizzy and depressed, and very much as if she'd made a mess of things.

David turned away and devoured his sandwich before talking again. And when he spoke, his words were bitter.

"What gives you the right to press me about my love life, when you're the one who's engaged?"

"Oh, David," Marie said, bringing her coat sleeve to her mouth and feeling as if she were going to burst into tears. "I have no fiancé. Not anymore."

David balled up his napkin and spun to face her in the moonless night.

Her eyes looked moist behind her glasses and her lower lip was trembling.

"No fiancé?" he asked, his voice a low vibrato.

She removed her glasses and shook her head.

And, with an overwhelming certainty, David knew he would have to kiss her—and kiss her as no man had before.

## Chapter Six

"I think I need to go home," Marie said, getting abruptly to her feet as David leaned toward her.

"Why?" David asked, springing off the blanket, his head still spinning from the wine.

She feigned a shiver. "It's getting cold out and I..."

Cold? At the moment, David felt anything but.

"...have to be at work early."

"But Marie," David said, putting his hands on her shoulders. "We were just getting started."

Boy, didn't she know it. Getting started all over again. Getting ready to fall right into his two masculine arms.

"Here," she said, stepping away so he couldn't touch her and stooping at the edge of the blanket. "Let me help you with this."

David ran his hands through his hair, trying to think of what to do next. Picking up the blanket? No way. This was not supposed to be happening, now that he wanted to take her in his arms and tumble her to the ground.

David stood by helplessly as Marie tugged the blanket out from under his feet and folded it neatly.

"Ready?" she asked, giving him a pleasant smile he thought better suited to one of her story hour attendees.

"Ready," he said, somehow imagining that the ride going home wouldn't be nearly as exciting as the one coming out here.

David stuffed another potato chip in his mouth as Caroline leaned a hip against his cluttered desk. Her little girl did have the chicken pox. And, because she was going to be mostly at home for the next two weeks, Caroline felt the need to come in for an hour to give David all the necessary instructions.

"Don't know what I did wrong," he said, between gobbles. "I mean, I thought you women were really into that romance stuff."

"We are," Caroline said with an indulgent half smile. "But not, maybe, if you fellows come on too fast."

"Too fast? This thing has been moving so slowly I swear I can hear those wheels scrape the pavement every time I see her!"

"Come now, David. Really, what's it been? One week?"

Caroline kicked off her heels and breathed an audible sigh of relief.

David perched a handful of chips in front of his mouth and paused.

"About that, I guess. But Caroline, you know how it is. Usually the girls are all over me!"

Caroline gave a hearty laugh, inched backwards and settled her rear on his desk.

"Kind of gets to your ego, huh?" she asked, swinging her legs freely as she sat there making a study of him.

But it wasn't his ego, really. It was something more like an itch. An itch he couldn't scratch and it was driving him crazy.

"I can't take it, Caroline!" he said, heaving himself forward and pounding his fists on either side of his head as it collapsed to the desk. "I'm not that strong a man!"

"Oh now, honey," she said, running her affectionate fingers through his hair, "from where I sit, you are made of steel."

David heard a nervous cough and looked up to find a startled Marie standing in the threshold to the back room.

"I just came..." she trailed off weakly, her face turning pink. She held up a bent pair of turquoise frames, apparently almost unable to finish. "...to redeem my unconditional guarantee."


"Slow down there a minute, child," Joanne said as Marie wheezed into the ladies' room sink. "I can't understand a word you're saying."

"Don't you see? I bent my frames on purpose. On purpose, Joanne! Just because I got to thinking I'd made a big mistake..."

She burst into sobs again and honked into a tissue.

"Made of steel! I swear, I'll never forget that woman's face as long as I live."

"Honey," Joanne said, lightly rubbing her back, "Don't you think it's possible you got it all wrong?"

"Wrong?" Marly snorted. "I don't think so. She was half naked, for heavens' sake!"

Joanne narrowed her eyes.

"Well, she'd already kicked off her shoes..."

Joanne hefted her large leather purse onto the counter. "You're going to be a mess introducing that touring book author. A real mess. Here," she said, her arm disappearing into her cavernous bag. "Let me see if I've got something in here that can help you."

"Joanne," Marie said sternly, lowering her slightly crooked glasses. "If it's one of those psychedelic drugs from the sixties..."

Joanne laughed and produced a roll of hard candies.

"Lemon or cherry?" she asked with a subtle smile.

Marie popped a cherry candy in her mouth and wished that all the men in the world were as easy to deal with as Joanne. She blew her nose again, then cleared her throat.

"So, how are things going with Chad?" she asked, surveying her ghastly reflection in the mirror. She'd have to redo the blush and the lipstick for sure, she thought, fumbling through her own pocketbook.

"Oh, honey, don't you worry about me and Chad. That old gray fox and I have an understanding."

"Oh?" Marie asked, applying a dab of lipstick.

"Yeah," Joanne said, her dark eyes twinkling. "He understands what I like and vice versa."

Marie chuckled and swept on a little blush, finally feeling half human. "It's taken me a while," she said, packing away her makeup in her purse. "But I guess I can now see why you found matrimony so distasteful."

"Distasteful?" Joanne asked, puckering up her lips and examining her own image in the mirror. "Heavens, did I say that?"

Marie slapped her on the arm. "You most certainly did! At least, that's how I took it."

"Well then, love," Joanne said, fiddling with her braid and pinching color into her cheeks. "Maybe you got that wrong, too."

"Joanne!" Marie said, her eyes sparkling with disbelief. "You're not—"

"I am," Joanne said with a cryptic smile.

Marie tugged on her bedtime socks, thinking about Joanne's remarks. She was certain the other woman wasn't telling her everything that was going on between her and Chad. At least their relationship had a chance. All this fantasizing about David Lake was getting out of hand. It was wonderful to imagine that he was Prince Charming, the gallant swain that romance novels were made of. But it would only be a matter of time before cold, hard reality hit.

David was sexy, attractive—yes. But Marie needed more. A person she could talk to. Somebody with whom she could share a passionate love of life. She'd never really had that with Cecil, or—goodness knows—with sexy Paul. With Paul, it had been all smoke and fire, until the whole thing had entirely burned out and Paul had gone on to someone else.

With Cecil—well, there wasn't exactly fire, but the two of them at least could carry on a conversation, even if they didn't always totally agree. Cecil simply worked too hard at being eccentric. And, to Marie, eccentric wasn't something you became, it was something you were—like it or not. But Cecil seemed to like the image of the "starving artist" very much. Organic foods and vegetarian cuisine were his mantra, but when no one was looking he was sneaking off for fast food burgers at the edge of town. Marie knew this because she'd found a whole store of paper wrappers wadded up under the front seat of his car.

If she'd applied half the investigative skill she used in tracking missing merchandise to dissecting her relationship with Cecil, she would have seen him for who he really was sooner. As it turned out, he'd been hiding more than the burger wrappers. He'd concealed his lust for another woman and the very important fact that he'd finally sold that incomprehensible book! He'd never even let her read it. Hardly a testament to the trust between them.

Marie nabbed the romance novel off her nightstand and settled back against the headboard.

She was curious to see what direction her favorite historical novelist, B. B. Knight, had taken the noble

MacMillan clan... and their ignoble forefathers. If there was anything that could take Marie's mind off her worries, it was a muscular man in a kilt.

David pushed the disconnect button on his cell phone for the third time in a row. She would kill him, that's what she'd do. He checked his watch and saw it was five past nine. Books & Bistro had just closed its doors, and Marie had been nowhere in sight.

"Went home early," Joanne had told him. And then she'd surprised him by slipping him Marie's cell number.

David wasn't sure what Marie had told Joanne about him, but from the elderly woman's encouraging reception, David suspected that she felt a whole heck of a lot better about him than Marie did at the moment.

Until he drew his final breath, David would be haunted by the total disillusionment—and shock—he'd seen in Marie's eyes. She hadn't stayed to hand over the glasses. Just turned tail and run like a frightened rabbit.

Caroline had advised him to go after her. But he'd known there was no way on earth he could have explained away what she'd seen right then. Better to give her time, he'd decided. Even though Caroline had huffed and somehow sided with Marie. Holy cow, Caroline had caused the problem! And there she'd stood, slipping her skyscraper shoes back on, telling him that he was the one making mistakes.

David inhaled deeply and tried Marie's number again. He was just about to hang up a fourth time when she answered.

"Hello?" she said, as his throat closed up. "Anybody there?"

"Marie, this is David. David Lake," he said, praying she wouldn't press *end call*.

Of course it was David Lake. How many other Davids did Marie know who sent shivers down her spine just from the sound of his voice?

"I know what you must think of me, but I wanted a chance to explain."

She wasn't speaking, so he plowed right ahead. "I know what you walked in on looked bad, but it wasn't what you thought at all. Holy cow, Caroline's my boss!"

"How convenient."

"Oh, no. It's like that," David stuttered. "She was just giving me some advice."

Marie wasn't altogether sure she wanted to hear this.

"Look, David, the picnic was nice and all, but forgive me if I say I've already figured you out."

"Think what you will, Marie, but none of it's true. I mean, yeah, maybe once..." Did he need a speech therapist or what? He couldn't seem to get words out and have them make sense. David ran a hand along the damp back of his neck. Thirty-five degrees out and he was sweating!

"Marie, a lot has changed about me that you don't know. You don't know me at all, in fact."

She knew him well enough and intended to keep it that way. More than she'd realized at first, Cecil had left her in a fragile state. Now was no time to go getting mixed up with a handsome optician who left her unable to see straight.

"David," she said calmly. "It's late, I'm tired, and I'm afraid I'm all talked out."

"Well, that's too bad," David said, his scowl almost visible through the phone, "because talking's precisely what I had in mind. Fun talk. Nothing heavy. Just you and me, a cup of coffee somewhere. We could get to know each other a little better."

Marie's heart skipped a beat. Hadn't she just been thinking...? No, she told herself, violently shaking her head. She wouldn't fall for it.

"Besides, I've been reading something I think you'd really like."

"Oh?" she asked, her damnable interest piqued. If there was any way to get to a bookstore manager, it was by talking shop. "What is it?"

"Now that wouldn't be fair for me to give away all my conversation in advance, would it? Let's just say you and I might have a lot more in common than you seem to think."

Marie bit her bottom lip, telling herself not to buy it. Not to be hopeful, stupid—or both. "I don't know," she hedged.

"One hour, one cup of coffee is all I'm asking."

Well, she thought, fanning her romance book out on her chest with a sigh, what would one cup of coffee hurt? Even the fourteenth-century heroine of the book she was reading had decided to give her dastardly hero another chance.

"When and where?" she asked, sounding resigned.

The whole staff of Books & Bistro pressed their noses to the frosty glass and watched as David held his cell phone high above his head and did a celebration dance around the gravel parking lot.

And he didn't even care what they thought.

# Chapter Seven

David pulled up to the small white house with the dormer windows and wicker porch swing, and smiled in reflection. Somehow it seemed just like her. All homespun and comfortable, but pretty and inviting. Its neat front walk was lined with tapered boxwoods, while the large red oak near the center of the yard filtered morning sunlight through its turning leaves. A vision of a tire swing hanging from one of the old oak's sturdy branches came to mind. But David quickly dismissed it and hurried up the steps to the house. He was ten minutes late already.

Marie checked her image in the hall mirror for what seemed like the hundredth time. If this was such a casual thing, then why did she feel like a schoolgirl about to entertain her first beau? She yanked the rubber band out of her hair, deciding the ponytail looked too perky. She was going to get better acquainted with David, not audition for the cheer-leading squad.

She adjusted the straps on her corduroy jumper, thinking maybe she'd tried too hard to look conservative. One of the sweater dresses would have been better. David had never been able to take his eyes off her when she'd been wearing one of those. Of course, David always seemed to check her out no matter what she was wearing, and in a strange way Marie found that extremely stimulating. No other man, including Paul, had seemed so totally smitten by her appeal.

The doorbell rang, nearly jolting her out of her shoes. She took a quick second look at the way her loose wavy hair fell about her shoulders, and decided it was okay. But, oh God, her glasses!

Marie lay a sweaty palm on the doorknob, knowing it was too late to do anything about those now.

"Hi!" she said, pulling back the door.

The crisp scent of autumn rushed past her, carrying his musk oil scent, and she nearly fainted.

"Hi," he said, one hand coyly tucked behind his back. He smiled and his eyes seemed as blue as the morning sky. "I brought you something."

"Oh, you shouldn't—" Marie started to protest, but when he whipped out a jumbo bag of candy-coated chocolates, she changed her mind.

"Why, thank you!" she said, hating herself for blushing. "How did you know I had a weakness?"

"All women..." David started to say, but he caught himself. Smart move, he chided himself. The playboy image is precisely what she's looking for.

He chuckled and shrugged his wide shoulders.

"Well, to hear Debbie tell it, all women love chocolate."

"Debbie?"

"My sister."

"Oh, the one who's getting married!"

"Ah, yeah. Right."

Marie smiled.

"Say," he said, motioning toward the door, "we seem to be letting an awful lot of heat out. Should we get going, or are you going to ask me in?"

Marie turned every shade of red on the spectrum, thinking he didn't know the truth in his words. Her internal combustion engine was fired up and running—right away with her reason.

"Oh, here," she said, "I'm so sorry. Yes, please come in while I get my coat."

David stepped through the threshold and into the sweetest-smelling house he'd ever been in. There was a lingering scent of cinnamon, fresh flowers, and—he swore—something that smelled just like gingerbread. For all intents and purposes, he could have stepped back in time and walked right into his grandmother's home in rural North Carolina.

"Nice place," he said, looking around. Although a bit cluttered, everything was neatly arranged. There were some nice pieces, antiques, David thought, but mainly just comfortable furniture that had seen a lot of living. "Real settled."

"Settled?" Marie asked, sticking one arm into her coat, as David walked over and hoisted the rest of it onto her shoulders.

"Yeah. Not much of a bachelorette pad, if you know what I mean. Reminds me of my grandma's house."

She pushed her glasses up on her nose and buttoned up her coat. "In a good way, I hope."

David's smile was genuine. "In a very good way, Marie," he said, his voice pleasantly husky. "I loved my grandma's house. You live here with your folks?"

"Mother died when I was young, my dad—last year," she said, taking pains to keep her eyes on her keys.

"Oh, I'm sorry."

"Well," Marie said forcing a brave smile. "Don't be too sorry for me. I've still got some pretty good memories of my mom, and my dad was a terrific father to all of us."

"All of you? How many are there?"

"Well," she said, seeming to brighten at the opportunity to show off her family. She crossed to the upright piano at the end of the living room and picked up a picture frame.

"This is Johnny. He's the oldest and has just gotten engaged to Meg. This was taken at their engagement party in July."

She pointed to a photo of another man who looked a lot like Johnny but wore a mustache. "This one's Mark. And this is my sister Jill with her husband Dan, and this one's my baby sister Teresa with her husband Jack."

Her sisters—one blond, the younger one brunette and resembling Marie—were pretty women. But, as far as David was concerned, Marie outshone them both.

"Quite an attractive bunch."

"We hold our own," she said, smiling proudly. "How about you? You have a big family?"

"Just me and Debbie." David gave her a wry smile. "She's the oldest, but you'd never know it."

"And your parents?"

"Dad's in banking down in North Carolina. Mom's made a career out of the Junior League."

"How wonderful she can volunteer."

Yeah, David thought. If only she'd spent a comparable amount of time with the only two children she had. If only his father understood that a man was worth more than the money he made—or in David's case, didn't make.

"Shall we go?" Marie asked, looking down at her watch. "I do need to be at work by noon, and it's almost ten-thirty."

"Your chariot awaits," David said, holding back the door. "Watch your step."

Which was precisely what Marie intended to do, especially since she had the sinking feeling that the rug was somehow going to get pulled right out from under her.

"Didn't know you owned a car," Marie said, sliding into his old Mazda.

He gave her a startled look and then burst out laughing. "Hey, the bicycle is mainly for work. It's close to where I live; I hate to think I'm polluting the environment just to go two blocks."

Uh-oh, Marie thought, red flag number one going up. This was Cecil talk. Not that she didn't believe in protecting the environment. It had been her, after all, who'd suggested Books & Bistro use recycled paper products. But something about the idea that David would have anything in common with Cecil Barnes made her faintly sick to her stomach.

"Glad you liked the chocolates," he said, changing the subject. "I'm a big fan myself."

Marie raised one eyebrow. A male chocoholic, now that was something. "Next you're going to tell me that you like Tater Tots, and devour potato chips by the handful."

David laughed and hung a left down the main street, leading to campus. "I am a bit of a junk food junkie," he said, looking sideways with a mischievous grin. "But please don't hold my gourmet ice cream against me."

Marie's mind painted a really naughty picture of her and a very naked David getting creative with a pint-size container on her kitchen floor.

She blinked, then leaned forward—instinctively jamming her hand under the car seat.

David pulled his car to a stop at one of the only two traffic lights in town.

"Mind telling me what you're doing?"

Marie slammed back in her seat, acutely aware of her blunder.

"Looking for rice cakes?" she said with a sheepish shrug.

David laughed so loudly that he didn't see the light change.

"Huh?"

He collapsed in hilarity again, white knuckles gripping the wheel.

"Light's green," she said, with a nudge.

"Oh, right," he said, straightening himself in his seat with another burst of laughter.

He put his car in gear, then pulled up to a nearby curb beside the *Cafe Ole Coffee Shop*.

David shut off the ignition, then turned to look at her.

"Now, why on earth would you think I'd hide rice cakes under my passenger seat?"

Marie sunk her chin below the collar of her coat.

"Wild guess?"

"That I'm a closet health nut?" David chuckled again. "No worries there, sweetheart."

"Come on," he said, scooting around the car and opening her door, "let's go in and get some coffee with plenty of white sugar. And cream."

Marie stayed, nailed to the passenger seat by his guileless eyes. What in the world had she been thinking? That he would hide an addiction to rice cakes, just as holistic Cecil had concealed his penchant for fast food?

David gave her a crooked smile and Marie's heart beat faster.

"Coming out?" he asked, his smile broadening, "or am I going to have to come in there and get you?"

Her heart beat faster still, just imagining what that might entail.

"No, it's all right," she said, composing herself. "I can manage."

David held out his hand, but she steadied herself against the car door instead and climbed out. No way was she going to touch him now. Now that her palms were slick and her cheeks hot pink.

David took her by the elbow anyway and helped her out of the car.

"Are you always this chivalrous?" she asked, "Or is it because I remind you of your grandmother?"

Marie caught a twinkle in his eye and sensed he was thinking something that she didn't care to know.

"You bring out the gentleman in me. What I can I say?"

"Ah, so you finally admit," she teased, as they crossed the sidewalk to the cafe, "that you're not always so gentlemanly."

"Guilty," he said, with a sheepish look as he held back the heavy glass door. "But I can promise you this. I've never, ever done anything a woman hasn't wanted me to do."

Marie swallowed hard and selected a table. Something about David made her believe that a woman would actually get down on her knees and beg for his manly attention.

Not her, she decided with a shake of her head. She was getting to know him, that was all. As a friend. But Marie hadn't had a male friend in—she didn't know how long. That was exactly her problem. She'd gone from one long-term relationship to the next. What she needed now was a breather, not a man who left her breathless.

"So, what would you like?"

Marie looked up into his vibrant blue eyes. Maybe this wasn't such a good idea, after all.

"Coffee," she said, realizing the waitress had appeared at their table. "Coffee and an orange scone, please."

"Scone?" David asked, with feigned indignation. He leaned in with a gravelly whisper, "Not nearly enough sugar."

David turned and directed his attention to their server. "I'll take coffee, too, with double cream. And bring me one of those gigantic cinnamon buns with the icing dripping all over it."

The waitress nodded, and started to turn.

"No, wait! Make that two!"

The waitress's face was an open question.

"Cinnamon buns."

"David Lake, every one of those perfect teeth is going to rot and fall out."

"Marie, now you're sounding like my mother! Have you ever tried those things? They're wicked with a capital W."

No, Marie thought. Wicked with a capital W was sitting right in front of her. She didn't know how he could really eat like that. But David Lake didn't appear to have one surplus ounce on his entire body.

"So, David," she said, trying to get things on a more intellectual tract. "Tell me more about that book you've been reading."

But somehow, it was terribly hard to think about that boring book, with the exciting Marie McCloud sitting right across from him. She looked cute in that strappy brown jumper, pulled over a tight-fitting shirt that David wished he could see more of. Her cheeks had that gorgeous glow and her eyes fixed on him in that manner that made his head spin. David noticed her glasses sat slightly off center.

Most likely thanks to that nasty dent right in the center of their bridge.

"I can still fix those glasses for you, you know."

"Huh?"

Marie brought a startled hand to the edge of her frames.

"Uh, I forgot they were... What I mean is, I can still see straight." No, that was baloney. "Fine, I mean. I can see just fine! The lenses weren't damaged at all."

"You sure about that?" he asked, reaching forward and gently lifting the glasses from her face. "Because usually when the frames get bent..."

He took the turquoise frames and turned them over and over in his hands before holding them up to the light.

"Now that *is* odd. Not a scratch on them. How did you say this happened?"

Marie blanched. "I, uh, it was the..."

"Looks almost like a child just—"

"Yes, that's it!"

She cowered, realizing her voice had risen about the buzz of the restaurant, and made an effort to speak more softly. "One of the kids at story hour—he bent my frames."

"Wow!" David said with surprise, as the waitress set down two steaming mugs. "Never realized your work was so dangerous."

Marie nervously stirred her coffee, wishing she knew what was going on behind those crystal blue eyes.

"Oh, not really so dangerous. You know kids get a little wound up at times. He didn't mean it, I'm sure."

"And the mother didn't even offer to pay to have them fixed?" David asked, dumping four packets of sugar in his cup. "I think that's awful."

"Well, what with the guarantee and all that, I figured, why make a big deal?"

David studied her as her spoon clinked repeatedly in her black cup.

"Don't you think you want to put something in there before you stir it?"

A nervous laugh caught in her throat. "I take mine black."

The waitress rescued her from further humiliation by bring their pastries.

"Well, anyway," David said, handing back her glasses, "if you want to drop by the shop later this week, I'd be happy to try to straighten those out for you—or replace them with another pair."

Marie was so flustered at the moment that all she could think of was downing her coffee and getting to work. Children's story hour? Heavens to Betsy, what had she done? Blaming some poor, innocent, imaginary little boy. When all the while it had been *her* pressing her flawless frames against the ladies' room sink counter!

"You feeling all right?" David asked, unrolling a bit of cinnamon bun and dipping it in his milky coffee.

"Fine, fine." Marie took a bite of scone, hoping she wouldn't choke. "Mmm, this is delicious."

"You sure you're okay? You look a little... hot."

Now that was the understatement of the year, David told himself. Marie McCloud always looked more than a little hot. No matter where she was, no matter what she wore, when she looked at him with those big brown eyes, she positively sizzled.

But she did look uncomfortable, sitting there going crazy with that rotating spoon. A little off balance somehow. Then she picked up her mug and drained one third of the coffee out of it before setting it back on the table.

"Well, it's true I haven't been feeling myself lately. Maybe there's something going around."

David nodded sympathetically. "Maybe you should take the day off. Grab a little R & R."

She looked over at him, and—for a brief second—seemed to be considering it.

"No, we have a staff meeting this afternoon. And I have book orders to review."

"Well, surely they'll understand if you—"

Marie stole a glance at her watch. "Oh my gosh, it's eleven-forty! David, we'd better get the check and get going."

Well, he thought, pulling out his wallet. He could never be accused of not trying.

The idea of a whole uninterrupted day with Marie McCloud tantalized David with all kinds of possibilities. He could create opportunities to get close to her and—

"Ready?" she asked, polishing off her coffee.

But, at that very moment, David feared that rising from the table would show her precisely how ready he was.

"Can you give me another minute?" he asked, stalling for time.

And then he called over the waitress and asked for a very tall, very cold glass of water.

# Chapter Eight

David pulled out of the Books & Bistro parking lot, thinking things had gone exceptionally well. There had definitely been some body-talking going on between them. And, no matter how abruptly Marie had wanted to leave, David couldn't help but believe that part of the reason she'd wanted to go had to do with her growing attraction to him. He'd seen it in her eyes, sensed it in the air between them at the outdoor picnic. Even that day in the park, there'd been a spark of something mixed with an admirable ire. Boy, she was a hot one. But impossible to pin down.

No, not impossible, David told himself. Nothing was impossible right up until the point you gave up trying.

What David needed, he decided, was a new angle. That book angle he'd been working on. He was sure that's what had been holding Marie back. Idle conversation and casual picnics weren't enough for a brainy woman like her. Cecil had been absolutely right. The mind link was what David needed to establish. He knew it was a little deceptive, given his honest aversion to what he'd been reading—one of Cecil's recommendations. But, in the end, it would hardly matter. He and Marie were meant for each other. David just knew it.

The literary connection would be just the beginning. After that, he was certain they'd find other things they could talk about. Other hobbies and ideals they shared. This was just too powerful, just too earth-shaking to mean nothing but sex.

David wanted more.

Now that he'd finally finished that damned book, all he'd have to devise was a creative way to...

David signaled for a turn then let out a cry. He slammed his palm into the wheel and honked merrily at an unsuspecting passerby, as he maneuvered a quick U-turn.

Today was definitely his lucky day.

Marie closed the cover of *Too Tempted Far Words* and let out an audible sound that was half pant, half sigh. She didn't even know people had that much fun back then. But it certainly had left the heroine smiling.

"Marie?"

She looked up and realized her coffee had gone cold.

David held up one of her fleece-lined gloves.

"You left this on the seat of my car. Thought you might be wanting it later."

What Marie would be wanting later had nothing to do with putting things *on,* she realized with a jolt.

Ever since page one hundred and seventeen, every third description of this book's hero had seemed better suited to David than a sixteenth-century nobleman. Right down to his enticing... oh, never mind.

"Thanks," Marie said, biting her lip. "Didn't even realize it was gone. It must have slipped out of my pocket."

"Don't worry about it," David said, brightening the room with his smile.

All afternoon, it had been pouring, the small cafe shadowed and gloomy from the rain outdoors. But suddenly, it was all warmth and sunshine in here and Marie regretted that her coffee break had ended and it was time to get back to work.

"I'm sorry, David," she said, standing. "But I've got a staff meeting in five minutes."

"And afterwards?"

"And afterwards, I've got inventory. Cash register receipts. A chance to review the coming week's schedule—"

"Excuse me," David said, clearing his throat. "And just where does the fun get penciled in?"

"Fun?" Marie asked, clutching her book to her chest as if he could see right through its very cover and know exactly what she'd been reading.

"Oh David, I don't have time for..."

But the way that he looked at her told her that she did.

"We never did get to discuss that book," he persisted.

"Oh right, the book!" she said, relieved to be on a safe subject. Nobody could shake Marie McCloud when it came to books. Now there was an area in which she felt confident.

"I could bring it by, if you want."

"By where?"

"By your house, of course. I've already finished the whole thing." And was that ever an accomplishment in his mind. "And I was thinking it would be great if you read it, too. Then we could discuss it."

Well, that was an intriguing proposition. As long as Marie could keep her mind on whatever he brought and her hands off the delivery man.

She tried to sound nonchalant. "I won't be home until after nine."

"Is ten o'clock too late, then?"

"Ten is fine," she said, feeling her whole world careen out of focus.

David showed up at ten sharp with—of all things— *Silence In The Trees.*

"A literary thriller?" Marie asked, trying hard not to remember that the author's previous work had been Cecil's favorite, and that this one featured a philosophical serial killer who was forever quoting Nietzsche.

"Why yes. Have you read it?"

"Not yet," she answered, an unexpected queasiness in her stomach.

"Well, great," he said, standing under the dim porch light, night sounds echoing all around him.

Marie had planned to ask him in, had straightened the house and whipped up a batch of store-mix brownies. But... *Silence In The Trees?* Her stomach clenched.

Marie knew she was supposed to be impartial. And she was, when it came to book store management. She studied demographics, knew her market, purchased what would sell in this little town. But when it came to her personal taste, Marie much preferred works with dialogue in quotation marks and no Nietzsche.

"Thanks, David," she said, feeling very much like she wanted to be alone.

"No problem." He smiled and backed into the darkness. "I'll be looking for you at my shop. Stop by and left me know what you think of the book. Oh, and I'll fix those frames."

Marie tossed *Silence In The Trees* onto the coffee table and sunk into the sofa, removing her glasses. Red flag number two, she thought, massaging her throbbing temples. David just might be a self-proclaimed environmentalist with a pretentious literary bent.

This was what she had feared was coming. The one-two punch at the end of her long day. The stark reality of life in the not-so-fast lane.

Well, who had she been fooling anyway? To think there'd be someone out there just like her had been ridiculous. Impossible. And in Covesville, impossible things weren't happening every day.

Marie waited a respectable two days, then decided to return *Silence In The Trees* to David. She'd read some of it—but she couldn't stand to have the book taking up space in her house one day longer.

If this was what David was into, he had far more in common with Cecil Barnes than Marie had ever dreamed of. The writer was a whiz at description—including painstakingly graphic portrayals of gruesome serial murders—but didn't care at all about romance. There was potential there. Such great potential, for something heated to develop between lead investigator Mona Malcom and the falsely accused Brad Billingsly. But nothing doing. Each protagonist seemed much too self-absorbed to attempt to peel the clothes off someone else. For heaven's sake! Was this considered entertainment?

Not in Marie's favorite stories, where good always triumphed over evil and love conquered all. Hey, if she wanted the bad news, she'd read the newspapers. Fiction was supposed to be about feeling better, about *forgetting*.

Well, forgetting was exactly what she intended to do. Forget all about those idealistic notions that made her want to believe David was more than a small town stud in tight-fitting jeans. That he—heaven forbid—might actually be the one! The one for what, for goodness sake?

Just because he pushed her buttons as no other man had, that didn't mean he was the right one for her. The right man, when he came along, would have a whole heck of a lot more going for him than a mesmerizing smile, melting blue eyes and a body to yearn for.

No! She was doing it again... remembering all the wrong things instead of focusing on the differences between them.

Despite his protests to the contrary, David was most certainly a ladies' man, one who'd never be contented with a bookworm like her. At least, not for the long term. She knew his game. It was the challenge that was driving him, that was all, but she wouldn't give in.

And if he actually liked that awful book... well, that was just more proof that David's vision of the world was one hundred and eighty degrees different from hers. Of course, that figured. After all, he'd made a point of mentioning that he came from a wealthy family where his mother had been able to stay home and dedicate herself to charity causes.

Marie's background had been the complete opposite. Hers had been an upbringing filled with blood, sweat and tears. And yet, despite the hardships, she wouldn't trade her experiences for anything. What she'd gone through had made her strong, capable of standing on her own. And, despite her girlhood fantasies, Marie knew she really didn't need a man to sweep her off her feet. Even though, at times... it still sounded awfully good.

No, but that was crazy. David Lake was not the sort who thought of ever after. He was more the here-and-now kind of animal. And she'd just have to keep him at bay.

Marie pushed through the door to the optician's shop, ready to fight. She'd just gotten off work and wanted to get this over with as quickly as possible, so she could go home, order a pizza and enjoy her juicy new novel in peace.

David's eyes sparkled when he caught sight of her. "Well, well, Miss McCloud!" he said, with a jovial smile. "Good afternoon! Be with you in just a second."

He seemed to be busy helping some college coed select a glasses case. Although to look at the young woman, practically panting at him, Marie could have sworn her interest was more in David's potential rigidity than in whether her case should be soft or hard.

Marie watched the girl giggle and tighten her arms to her chest so that her cleavage would be more visible. Although Marie wasn't sure just how much more visible it could get. The woman's breasts were practically falling out of her low-cut lycra leotard.

Her nylon shorts were cut high on her thighs, which Marie was sure David had noticed were much more shapely than hers. Though Marie didn't think she had a bad figure, it certainly looked nothing like *that*. Poor child must have to sweat through an aerobics class at least three times a day to maintain a body that perfect.

She leaned forward, her loose blond hair swinging above her ample breasts, and blew David a kiss.

"Ciao, sweetie," she said, doing her best to sound sensual. "Don't forget to call when you're ready for that workout."

Marie stepped forward and dropped her books onto the counter with an attention-getting thud.

Cat-like green eyes turned in her direction. "Here to get your glasses fixed?" the young woman asked with a purr.

"Actually," Marie said, removing her glasses and leaning over so she could grip David by the elbow. "I came in to see my very good friend, David Lake."

Holy cow, what was this? David looked from Marie to the customer and then back again. The threat of competition? He wished he'd thought of that earlier.

"If you don't mind," Marie said, turning her steely gaze on Candy. "David and I have something to discuss..."

"Whatever," Candy said with a tug at her low neckline and a careless shrug of her shoulders.

"You got my number, babe," she said to David, as she turned and began a hip-swiveling promenade out the door.

Marie had the strangest look on her face. And until she grinned, David didn't realize she was about to burst out laughing.

"David!" Marie said, catching her breath. "Don't tell me you find that kind of blatant sexuality attractive!"

"No," David said, looking deep in her eyes. "I like the more understated kind."

She inhaled and lifted his book off the counter, forcing herself to remember her mission. "I brought back *Silence In The Trees,*" she said, striving to ignore her feeling of embarrassment. "Although I hate to admit—"

"Marie," David broke in, setting both hands down in front of her, "I hope you didn't think that Candy—"

"Candy?"

"The girl who was just in here." David actually blushed. "I just wanted you to know... I mean, she's an aerobics instructor at the gym where I work out. That's all there is to it, I swear."

Marie lowered her glasses. "I'm not so sure she knows that."

"No, but she will. Trust me," David said, lifting his hands and coming out from behind the counter.

She pivoted to hold his gaze and backed right into a display case.

"And just how are you planning on breaking the news?"

"I'm planning," David said, closing the distance between them in two long strides, "on telling her I'm involved with someone else."

Marie's heart raced and her skin went all damp and clammy. This was *not* why she'd come in here.

"Well, now that you have the book..." she said, trying to inch away.

But David stepped forward and pinned her to the counter with two strong arms.

"Marie," he said, looking into her eyes, his heated breath warming her skin. "I've got something to tell you."

*Oh, no you don't,* she wanted to say. Hoping to find some way, any way to stop the sweet words she feared would come, melting her more than the desire in his eyes.

Marie knew she should turn. Knew she should run. But instead, all she could do was stand up on tiptoes and stop his confession with a kiss.

David nearly toppled backwards when the blissful cotton candy of her mouth melted against his lips. She was kissing him! And didn't it feel good...

He responded with all the erotic skill he had, lightly parting her lips with his. It only made him want to beg for more.

Marie nearly swooned in his arms, grateful that his strength would support her. His kisses were hot and sensual. And persuasive. Oh, how she wanted to go where his touch promised he would lead.

David's hand slid under the front of her coat, found her breast, and stroked it.

Oh God, she was going to die of pleasure right then and there. And then he held her closer and she knew she wanted to live long enough to taste his heaven.

There was the light tinkling of a bell, and Marie tried to pull back from his desperate kiss.

"David," she said, as he brought her closer still, "I hear bells."

"Mmm, sweetheart," he said, nuzzling her neck. "Me too, me too."

Suddenly the bell sounded again. Only louder this time, and David broke contact.

"Is this any way to run a business?" Caroline asked, her hands on her hips.

"Of course not," David answered, taking Marie by the hand. "But now that you're here, Marie and I are going to take this business home."

# Chapter Nine

"You're going to lose your job!" Marie yelped, as David pulled her down the sidewalk.

"Yeah," David said, sweeping her into his arms. "And what a way to go!"

His hot mouth fell upon hers as his muscular arms pressed into her back, holding her so close she swore they were melting together. Particularly since she was wearing this heavy coat!

"David," Marie said, pushing back on his shoulders, "people are staring."

A group of college students with backpacks were waiting at the crosswalk and turned to gape, wide-eyed at the spectacle they were making of themselves.

David shouted at them with a frisky wave of his arm.

"Hey! You kids need glasses—there's an optician's shop right there!"

Marie burst into a giggle and buried her head in his shoulder.

"You," she said, whacking him on his backside, "are impossible."

"Spank me again," he said with a naughty grin, "I liked it."

Liked it? Oh my, she had liked it too. She was enjoying the sexual playfulness between them, without a trace of her usual inhibition.

"Come on," he said, securing an arm around her waist. "My car's over there."

"Car?" Marie asked, a little disappointed she wouldn't be treated to another bicycle ride. "But I thought you biked in. Good for the environment and all that."

David grimaced. Well, hey, it had sounded good at the time. Very Cecil-like. And Cecil, it was apparent, knew all about women like Marie. When David had gone back to Books & Bistro to thank him for his reading suggestions, he'd been told that Cecil had run off to New York with some girl writer half his age. The man had probably established that mind link he'd been talking about. David guessed that when it came to intelligent women, Cecil definitely knew his stuff.

"Ah yeah, right," David said, sliding his key into the passenger door. "Environment's definitely a top priority. Greenspace and all that."

"Greenpeace?" Marie asked, looking up as she adjusted her seat belt.

David smiled and shut the door. Boy, he'd have to watch what he said with her. She clearly knew more about all this than he did.

A frigid burst of wind reddened David's face as he scooted around the car.

"David," Marie said, as he climbed in and started the engine. "Your teeth are chattering. You really shouldn't have gone out without a coat."

Maybe not. But in his hurry to rush past Caroline, picking up his belongings had been the last thing on his mind.

"I'll be all right," he said, flipping on the heater. "At least until my boss catches up with me."

"What about your boss?" Marie asked, as they pulled away from the curb and headed towards campus. "Do you think she'll really let you go?"

"I doubt it." David eyed the digital car clock. "Look, it's almost six anyway. Caroline can just as easily close the shop as I can."

"Yeah, but how do you know that—after today—she won't change the locks?"

David chuckled. "Well, you can be sure she'll be mad at first. Caroline has a temper. But after a while, and especially after she's talked to Jim, she'll calm down and forgive me."

"Jim?" Marie asked, relieved to at last be able to unbutton her sweltering coat.

"Caroline's husband. A true romantic."

"Really?"

"Sure. He's a screenwriter."

"No kidding?" She wriggled her arms out of her coat one at a time. "What does he write?"

"Romantic comedy, of course." David flashed a big smile. "We could sure give him a few pointers."

Marie adjusted her glasses, hoping he was joking.

"Hey," David said, patting her arm. "Don't look so worried. I'm only kidding!"

She let out a soft breath, then sat bolt upright.

"Oh my gosh, David," she said, bringing her hands to her face, "I left my book in there."

*"Silence In The Trees?* Hey, don't worry about it. I'll just pick it up tomorrow."

"Not your book, mine!"

"Well, what's the big deal? I can bring it to you."

The big deal, the very big deal, was that the book Marie'd left at the optician's shop was *Check It Out,* a romance about a small town librarian who, thanks to the local physician, happily finds the cure for all her libidinal ills.

"Besides," David said, laying a firm hand on her thigh. "Something tells me that—this evening—neither of us is going to have much time for reading."

"David," Marie said, as he stood fumbling with his key at the door to his upstairs apartment. "I think we might be taking this a little fast."

Fast? Oh, no. David could practically hear the mental brakes grinding to a halt.

"We can take it at any speed you want," he said, his key finally engaging in the lock. He looked at her reassuringly.

"Listen, Marie, I'm not the kind who's going to pressure you into anything, if that's what you're afraid of."

She shivered a little. David pressuring her was not the trouble. It was the way that she couldn't seem to keep her hands off of *him* that had her worried.

Against her better judgment, Marie nodded and stepped into the lion's lair. A quick image of him on all fours on the floor of Books & Bistro burned through her mind, and she shivered again.

"Nice place," she said, looking around at the living area, sparsely furnished with odds and ends. It was all one room, with a galley kitchen at the far end. Marie looked at the large platform bed in the corner, then looked quickly back to David.

"Not much furniture. Mostly Grandma's attic, if you know what I mean. But I make do."

He grinned and she felt all hot and cold at the same time.

"Here," he said, lifting the coat she had lightly draped over her shoulders when she'd exited the car, "let me hang this up for you."

David reached over and hooked her coat on a rack by the front door, then took her by the arm.

"Come on," he said, his voice as smooth as whiskey, "let me show you around."

"There's more?" she asked, catching her breath as his hand slid down her sweatered arm and felt for her palm.

Marie tugged at the front of her dress, suffocating in its ribbed tightness.

"If you're getting too warm..." David said, looking down at her in a way that seemed to stop time.

She counted the heartbeats drumming loudly in her ear. When she got to three, David reached up and brought his free hand to her face.

Her heart raced past four, and, before she knew it, she was pressing seven. If she got to ten, something told her, she would not be able to stop whatever it was they were about to be doing.

"Marie," he whispered, as she counted eight... then nine....

David leaned in for a kiss.

"Oh!" Marie shouted, stepping backwards and dropping his hand.

"What is it? What's wrong?"

He looked earnestly into her eyes and placed both hands on her trembling shoulders.

She squeezed her eyes shut—hard. But in her imagination, it wasn't David that she saw. Only Cecil. Cecil and Paul, the two of them throwing their heads back in hilarity at how easy she was.

"You think," she asked softly, as her eyes blinked open, "we could open a window?"

"A window?" David stood upright and scratched the back of his head. "Sure, sweetheart, anything you want."

"Do you call all your women sweetheart?" Marie asked, nabbing a magazine off a cluttered end table and fanning her face.

"Beg pardon?"

"Sweetheart."

"Yes, dear—" he said, drawing closer, the fire in his eyes seeming to reignite.

"No, no," Marie said, pushing him back. "Answer the question."

David frowned. "Now, what would that be?"

"Do you," she asked, blowing out a hard breath and tugging at her dress again, "call all your women sweetheart?"

David stopped for a moment, as if to think, then walked to the window and threw it open wide.

"First," he said, as he slipped back behind her and linked his arms under her chest, "let's get this straight."

Marie bit her lip, as his hand brushed her hair and his heated breath tickled her nape.

"There *are* no other women. There have been no other women—ever since I first laid eyes on you."

He lowered his lips to her neck and trailed kisses to her ear.

"David—" Marie said, wishing he would stop and then wishing he wouldn't.

She let out a cry of half surprise, half pleasure as he turned her around slowly. His hungry mouth fell upon hers and ravished her lips, moving down swiftly to the soft, vulnerable spot at the base of her neck.

"David—" she groaned, as the magazine she'd been holding fell to the floor.

David pulled back, his hair disheveled, passion in his eyes.

"Oh, Marie. Baby. Sweetheart. You make me crazy. So totally crazy. But I promised... I know I did. If you want me to stop, tell me now." He sighed. "Because another minute or two of this and I don't think..."

Marie ran her sweating palms through her long, loose hair, knowing exactly what he meant. She had no business being here, putting herself in such a compromising position with a man who...

Her eyes dropped to the floor.

... reads *Publishers Weekly!*

"What's this?" she asked, swooping down like a raven and pulling the magazine off the carpet.

David swaggered back a step and straightened his shirt collar.

"Oh, it's just one of those book-biz magazines I subscribe to."

Marie flipped the *Publishers Weekly* over in her hand, but saw no address label.

David snatched back the magazine and smiled between his teeth.

"Not that I actually subscribe to this one. Gotta cut costs somewhere. Bought this issue at the newsstand."

She lifted one eyebrow. He was acting very suspicious. *Publishers Weekly* cost twice as much at the newsstand.

But, why oh why, should that surprise her? It appeared that all the men who read that rag had something to hide.

Red flag number three—or was it four, by now?—went up the pole.

Marie paled. Seeing red, she realized, made even the most mentally challenged of animals want to run.

Without another word, Marie walked over and grabbed her coat off the rack.

A befuddled David raced toward her. "Wait! What happened? What did I do?"

"I don't even know," she said, opening the door. "Guess that's the point." She walked out.

David stood there in utter disbelief, his tiny apartment still resonating from the sound of the slamming door.

"Thanks a lot Cecil," he said, chucking the *Publishers Weekly* into the trash.

And then he bolted out the door and sprinted after her.

Marie was crying so hard she couldn't see two feet in front of her. This was it. Absolutely it. With the exception of her romance heroes, from this point forward all men were off limits.

After all she had done to build a life, these—cavemen came along and scattered it to stones. Loving Paul was an innocent mistake, her first wide-eyed romance, so she hardly blamed herself—even at this point—for falling for him.

By the time she'd met Cecil, she should have known better. At twenty-seven, she wasn't exactly an innocent anymore. But, for all her savvy, she might as well have been Little Red Riding Hood.

And now, here was David—the man with the irresistible eyes who told such nice lies. First there was that little story about the bike. Environmental awareness—hah! She was sure now it had been a ploy to get her close to his admittedly perfect body.

And then, all that nonsense about literary fiction and the obviously unread copy of *Publishers Weekly.*

For all Marie knew, David probably didn't read anything without a centerfold.

She pulled herself to a stop at the corner near the familiar display of lights. Books & Bistro's elegant awning stood out among the group of shops that lined the outdoor mall.

David raced through the darkness, wondering where on earth she'd gone. He ran to the corner and frantically called left and right, before deciding to head back to the mall. If she'd gone anywhere, it had to be the bookstore. Her car would be there, at least.

David crossed the street and picked up speed, his toned thighs swinging into motion.

*What had she been thinking,* he asked himself, his head pounding as he ran.

He maintained his speed, crossing the second street, which, fortunately, was free of traffic. His panic-stricken eyes continued to search side streets.

What if she'd wandered off? What if she'd gotten lost? In Covesville?

David stopped at the crosswalk, acknowledging the absurdity of the notion. He was gasping for air, leaning forward to catch his breath, when he looked up and saw her disappearing into her car.

Oh, hell, no!

David ignored the Don't Walk sign and bolted into traffic, dodging angry drivers as several cars nearly collided, screeching to a halt in the middle of the busy intersection.

But by the time he got to the parking lot, all that remained of Marie were her tail lights fading in the night.

# Chapter Ten

David kicked open the door and entered the optician's shop, scowling.

"Good morning to you, too," Caroline said from behind the counter. "Good thing my husband Jim likes the same ball teams you do, or you'd be out on your rear."

David motioned her away and stormed toward the coffeepot.

"I mean it, David! What if I hadn't been here to lock up last night? Would you have done the wild thing right in the center of the floor with a million"—she gestured to the mirrored walls of frames—"eyes on you?"

"Don't be cute, Caroline," he said, filling his mug.

"Oh, so I get it," she said, stepping around the counter and walking over with her own mug. "She blew you off, did she? Got you all hot and bothered, then—"

"You know," he said, bringing his coffee to his lips, "sometimes you just don't know where to stop."

"No, David," Caroline said, slamming her mug onto the table. "You don't know where to stop! Has it ever occurred to you that this is a business? That maybe one of our clients could have walked in here with a five-year-old child when you were in the middle of your amorous romp?"

David dropped his head, knowing she was right. It had been reckless of him, foolish. Different, if he'd had the foresight to draw the blinds and lock the doors...

"All this talk about Marie!" Caroline shouted walking back into her office and then returning with a book. "Marie, Marie, Marie. But you can't seem to figure out what she wants."

David brought a hand to his aching head and massaged his brow with his fingers.

"Here," Caroline said, thumping something hard into his chest. "Sally's better now, so take the day off. Do some serious reading."

"What's this?" he asked, staring down at the maroon cover.

David took the paperback in his hand and read the blurb before flipping it back over. For an inane little romance about a small-town librarian with the hots for the local doc, *Check It Out* displayed some pretty steamy artwork.

"Don't know who left it here," Caroline continued, "but it's good. I've read it. Maybe you should, too."

As David fanned through the pages, hoping for more suggestive artwork, a receipt fluttered loose and butterflied to the floor.

"Books & Bistro?" Caroline asked, snatching it off the carpet before David could even bend at the waist.

Caroline shook her head with a wry smile. "Now, I wonder who on earth this belongs to?"

Marie collapsed on the sofa and lifted the ice pack to her swollen eyes. If the puffiness didn't go down soon, she'd have to go in to work anyway. It was bad enough she'd called to say she'd be late. With Thanksgiving next week, Books & Bistro was under the gun to prepare for the pre-Christmas purchasing frenzy. And, with so many of her employees taking leave for next week's holiday, that meant that this Friday was the deadline she'd decided to go by. If she could get everything done and organized as she'd planned, then maybe even she would get a chance to enjoy some turkey and sweet potato casserole in peace.

It was draining enough for Marie to host the meal for her sisters and their husbands, plus her brothers Johnny and Mark and their significant others. Last thing she needed on top of that was work stress to face the next day.

Of course, when Marie was being honest, she didn't really mind having everyone over as much as she pretended. There was something comforting in having the flock gather and knowing she was still—in some small way—in charge of the fold. She had been the one left with the family homestead, after all. So it was up to Marie, as the eldest, to uphold family tradition.

The only part of the tradition she didn't savor was her brothers' good-natured ribbing about her single status. She was sure to get an earful this year, now that Cecil had blown right out of her life like an autumn leaf caught up in a gale.

High winds pounded her front door screen and sent it rattling in its frame. The gustiness of central Virginia's fall was upon them, and it'd soon be time to bring in the porch swing, lest it get carried off somewhere far over the mountain one night while she was sleeping. The weatherman had predicted snow on the heels of the frigid front that was blowing in from Canada. Just as long as it held off until Friday, Marie thought, it could snow all it wanted. Wasn't often they got a white Christmas in these parts, and white Thanksgivings were rarer still. Snow here in November would be the talk of the town, and that would suit her just fine. One less reason for her brothers to focus on talking turkey about the obvious lack of a man in her life.

David ordered a decaffeinated coffee and carried his book to the high bar running the length of the long glass wall that separated Books & Bistro's interior cafe from the wrought-iron tables on the sidewalk outside.

Not a soul was out there. It was no wonder, David thought, as the wind gusted and blew two metal chairs to the ground.

The cold was coming, and David was glad. He was a winter sports fan, and because he had grown up in Asheville, quite an accomplished skier. There was something about a mountain lodge with a roaring fireplace after a long day on the slopes. Of course, it helped if you had someone to share it with. And, this time, he wasn't thinking about Bitsy, the chair lift attendant.

David sighed and cracked open the book. He was curious to see why Marie had been so upset about leaving it behind. Doubly interested because the style of the cover looked strikingly similar to the book he'd caught her reading over coffee just last week. Maybe Cecil had recommended the wrong approach. In fact, maybe Marie got enough of intellectual literature and grim best-sellers working here. She probably read books like this to relax. Nothing wrong with that.

David dove right into the prologue, his eyebrows shooting skyward.

Holy cow, he thought, marking his place and pausing to remove his pullover sweater. He had a feeling he'd be able to get into this.

Marie was just dropping her keys into her purse and stepping up onto the curb at Books & Bistro, when she came to an abrupt halt. Her eyes had to be playing tricks on her.

She removed her glasses and wiped them on her coat lapel before putting them back on again.

*Oh, my.* She just stood there, her feet rooted to the ground, her cheeks turning pink from the icy air.

There at the counter of the cafe sat David Lake in all his glory, reading... *reading...* her book!

Marie blinked twice as David lowered his hand to the counter, nabbed a paper napkin, then wadded it up against his brow.

He was so engrossed in the book he didn't even see her walk in, and right up to the stool where he sat.

"Were you planning on reading it first, and then giving it back?"

David raised his eyes, then nearly fell off the stool.

"Hey! Whoa—Marie!" he said, standing and slamming shut the book. "What a surprise!"

"A surprise, David? I work here." She looked him up and down, trying not to remember how good he'd felt pressed up against her. "What's your excuse?"

"I, ah, was returning your book," he said, thrusting *Check It Out* in her direction.

"It looks used," she said, taking the book but keeping her eyes on his.

David racked his brain, trying to recall the very careful plan he'd concocted on the way over here, but his mind swirled with visions of adventuresome librarian Judith Just enjoying her first complete examination by the probing Dr. Robert Right.

"Well?" Marie asked, tapping one beautiful foot on the floor. He studied that beautiful foot and her delicate ankle, and then his gaze moved up that long sweep of leg—which went on and on and didn't stop until it hit that hint of hemline just above her knees.

"I... uh." David cleared his throat.

"I think you already said that."

"Yes, well..."

He choked on air as she unbuttoned her coat. He noticed she was wearing another one of those sweater dresses that showed off her curves so well.

"I was waiting." David clenched his fists and dug his fingernails into his palms. "Waiting for you to get here."

He smiled through gritted teeth, and looked for all the world like a naughty boy who'd been caught with his hand in the cookie jar.

"Well, here I am," she said, unable to keep her gaze off the warm gleam in his eyes, the broad musculature of his chest... the snug fit of his faded denim jeans.

"Well, there you are," he said, motioning to the book he'd already placed in her hands.

He shuffled his feet and glanced out the window. "I hope you're not still mad about last night. Because if you are—"

"David," she stopped him. "It wasn't you, necessarily."

He inhaled deeply and his chest swelled, the taut muscles rippling beneath cotton.

Marie blinked and continued. "I mean, in some ways it was. But look," she said, trying hard not to. Why, oh why, did her eyes keep roving over him? "What I mean is, there's been so much going on in my life, and if you can't be honest with me—"

"Honest?" He folded his arms in front of his broad chest and knitted his brow. "Just what is it you think I've done to deceive you?"

"You tell me," she said, clutching her book to her bodice.

David looked positively stupefied.

"Does this have something to do with *Publishers Weekly?*"

She stood motionless, a hard look in her eyes beneath those charmingly tilted frames.

"Well, look, Marie," he said, giving a little laugh. "If that's all it is, I can explain. Not that I really understand why a simple little magazine would cause such a reaction..."

"It's just that it all started when Cecil—"

"Cecil?!"

"Sure, yes. Cecil, you know—"

"I know damn well who Cecil is, but I thought you said you didn't."

"Didn't I? I mean, no, I don't. Just a little—"

"Are you and Cecil in this together somehow?" she asked, eyebrows arching.

"Together? Wait. Whoa. I don't think you're getting-"

"Oh, I'm getting everything just fine. I might not be from your sophisticated background, David. But I didn't just fall off the turnip truck. You and Cecil devised some kind of plan, didn't you?"

Plan? Holy cow, what was happening here? This whole thing was spinning way out of control. He'd never seen her so furious.

"You hit on me, get me out of the way, so he can run off to New York with Diane."

"Diane? No—"

"Good job, David. Bravo," she said, a cold dismissal in her eyes."What with your talent, maybe you should join Cecil in New York. Hear they're in need of actors there."

"Marie, please."

She turned, and he placed a hand on her shoulder.

She looked back and narrowed her flaming eyes. "You lay one more hand on me, David Lake, I'll call security.

Now, I've got a life to lead," she said, striding away. "I'm sure you've got one waiting for your somewhere, too."

## Chapter Eleven

Mark looked over his shoulder and called back into the house. "Hey, Marie! There's some turkey with a bird on your doorstep!" She didn't answer.

"Just kidding, pal," Mark said, giving David a slap on the arm. "Come on in."

"Oh!" Meg, John's fiancée, rushed over. "You must be the guy! Marie told us last month she was getting married, but we all knew—-just knew—it couldn't be to that old boring Cecil!"

Despite her willowy frame, Meg looked pixie-like with her bridge of freckles and short red hair. "Johnny," she called, leaning back into the living room. "Oh, John-boy, come here!"

A tall, muscular man with jet-black hair appeared from around the corner, his dark eyes widening with surprise. "Well, hey there! You must be David."

"How did you know his name?" Meg questioned, swatting her fiancé on the rump.

"Talked to him on the phone."

David shifted the heavy turkey pan uncomfortably in his hands.

"Here, let me take that." A pretty ponytailed blonde with apple-dumpling cheeks appeared and lifted the roasting pan out of David's hands. "Honey," she said, talking to the lanky fellow behind her, "this is David, Marie's fiancé."

"No, wait!" David held out his hand.

But a dark-haired woman about an inch shorter than Marie walked over and used the opportunity to slip off one arm of his coat. "Your true love's here," she sang back into the kitchen in a lilting voice, before yanking the other arm free, then carrying his coat to the closet.

"What in the world is all the..." Marie strode into the front hall and froze, as an extremely tall brown-haired guy materialized at her back.

"You must be Jack. Jack Wagner," David said, stepping around Marie and stretching his hand out toward Teresa's husband. "Carolina basketball, right? ACC Championship year."

Jack gave a modest grin and nodded his big, square jaw.

David knew he'd recognized the face.

"Would somebody—*anybody*—mind tell me what's going on here? And just who let *him* in?" Marie shouted, as a flushed David turned to face her.

Mark quietly backed away, as the others appeared to decide whether or not they wanted to be discreet, or stay and watch the action.

"Well, I think," Meg said, tugging on Johnny's arm, "that we should all go and see what's cooking in the kitchen, and leave these two lovebirds alone."

"Good plan, sweetie," Johnny said, leaning over and planting an affectionate kiss on her cheek. "Especially since," he whispered in her ear, but not quite softly enough, "I'm the one who asked him to bring the turkey!"

Marie gave her brother an accusatory glare, but he just took Meg's arm and ignored her as he exited the room.

"Wow," David said, bringing his hands together in a clap, "what a great family you have."

Marie blinked behind her perfectly straight frames. "All right David, the truth. Just what are you doing here, and just how did you finagle a dinner invitation from my unsuspecting little brother?"

She looked so beautiful standing there, wonderfully domestic with flour dusting her bright red cheeks, her sensuous curves hugged ever so tightly by a full-length, green print apron. Those mesmerizing brown eyes and spectacular lashes flashing behind... wait!

"You got them fixed!" David blurted out. The surprise waned to disappointment when he realized that meant she'd taken them to someone else.

"Don't look so crestfallen," Marie said with a little shake of her head. "Though you may not be my type where romance is concerned, I didn't toss you over for another optician."

David instinctively stepped one inch closer, but she inched back.

"Caroline replaced the frames for me. No charge."

"Caroline?" David asked, startled. "But she didn't say a word." And, blast it all, she knew first-hand all the agony David had gone through since last week when Marie had shut him out of her life.

"Of course not," Marie huffed. "Caroline apparently has a deeper sense of loyalty than my traitor brother!"

Johnny, who had stuck his head into the foyer and was about to come get something, suddenly changed his mind and disappeared down the back hall.

"Oh, don't be too hard on Johnny. He just happened to pick up the land line. And, after all the times you'd slammed it down in my ear—"

"Now, don't you go defending my brother!" Marie said, taking one big step in his direction.

"No, I wouldn't dream—"

"And don't," she said, coming closer and thumping him on the chest, "go sharing your dreams—or fantasies, as they may be—about us being engaged with my family!"

David looked into her eyes, all fire and ice, and swore he felt his adam's apple melt.

"I didn't," he squeaked, then cleared his throat.

"So, is this the way it's going to be, then?" she asked, stepping up to him so her hairline was level with his shoulders. "More dyed-in-the-wool, bald-faced lies?"

She tilted her chin upward, set both hands on his shoulders, and gave him a rude push backwards. "Get out of my house!"

"Now, Marie," her sister Jill burst in. "Is that any way to treat the man you've pledged yourself to for eternity?"

Marie gritted her teeth and made some kind of snarling sound David couldn't identify. "For the last time—"

Jill laid a soothing hand on David's arm and a peace-making arm around Marie's shoulder. "Come on now, kids," she said, forcing a brilliant smile. "It's Thanksgiving. Let's all try being a little grateful for what we've got, huh?" She gave Marie a light squeeze, patted David affectionately, then walked into the arms of Dan, who'd been watching from the sidelines.

"Hello!" Marie screamed. "Hello, I know you're out there!"

David watched in amazement as heads popped out from around door frames and the rest of her siblings emerged from their hiding places with guilty looks.

"Really, guys," Marie scolded, "I thought you all had outgrown that nonsense by the time I was seventeen."

"Not quite," Mark said with a grin. "And, boy, did we see some good stuff! What was that fellow's name? Big guy you took to the prom?"

To Marie's relief, Johnny walked over and popped Mark on the head with a rolled-up newspaper. Just like Mark to make trouble. It was the first Thanksgiving in years that he hadn't brought home a girl, and his boredom was showing already.

"Soup's on!" Meg called, approaching from the kitchen. David had thought one was missing when he'd counted eavesdropping heads. No, two. David looked around. Where was Jack?

As if in answer to the question, Jack came out of the dining room. "Where shall we seat our guest?" he asked tactfully.

It annoyed Marie no end that she apparently had no say in whether or not David was staying for dinner, even though she was hosting it.

Not only that, but then everybody squabbled over where he would sit. Jack wanted to talk basketball, while Teresa wanted a detailed story about how Marie and David met. Mark wanted to discuss all the best ski resorts. Meg had grown up in North Carolina, and Johnny, the surgeon, was suddenly eager to hear all about some new lens-making procedure from David.

Marie sighed and cleared the salad plates, relieved that David had been seated at the opposite end of the table, but still not entirely sure she liked him occupying her father's chair. She walked to the kitchen, as a round of laughter exploded at her back, and the thought occurred to her that she might as well not be here at all.

She deposited the plates in the sink, then felt the rush of revelation. Of course! It was so obvious, she hadn't even seen it. As much as she loathed him being here, as desperately as she'd been trying not to meet his gaze, David was actually rescuing her.

For once in the past eight years, Marie was going to be able to enjoy a Thanksgiving dinner in peace. No probing questions, no ribbing. Done. It was settled. She was engaged! And now the spotlight was on David, not her.

Marie released a deep breath and let go of a lot of tension with it. If David was happy to play along, as he seemed content to do, then why not her? Get through this annual holiday. Get back to work, then move on. All she needed was a little more cooperation from David, and then after a couple more weeks she'd tell her siblings the engagement was off. With her track record, they'd certainly believe that.

Marie squared her shoulders and walked to the swinging door that led to the dining room. "Oh, David," she said, peeping through the door, her voice all sugar-sweetness. "Honey, could you come in here and help me with the turkey?"

"Carve it, you mean?" he asked, feeling his blood rush to his feet. David knew what that would require: long, sharp knives—or at least one. And one was all it would take, with a woman as riled as Marie. She'd hardly spoken to him all evening. Had barely turned her eyes upon his. And, when she had, he'd seen nothing more there than utter disregard.

David excused himself from the table and walked toward the kitchen, believing, at least, there was safety in numbers. Her whole family seemed to like him. And, boy, what a nice bunch they were. His family's dinners in Ashville had never been like this. No, instead of warm exchanges and laughter, they'd been filled with financial figures and boredom. He and his sister Debbie had never gotten a word in edgewise, and were always dismissed the moment they had finished their dinners.

"You called?" he asked, as the swinging door closed at his back.

"David," Marie said, holding up a long, gleaming knife. "I have a proposition."

David swallowed past the lump in his throat. "Oh, yeah?" he asked, his voice suddenly squeaky as a thirteen-year-old's.

"You and I are engaged," she said, digging the knife into the breast of the turkey and slicing off a chunk.

"Okay," he said, making no effort to move from where he was.

"Come over here, will you?" she said, motioning with the knife. "I don't want to shout it, for heaven's sake."

David steeled himself and took a few steps forward.

"What's wrong with you, anyway?" Marie asked. "One minute you're the loving fiancé, the next you act as if you're afraid..." She looked down at the knife which she'd thrust back into the turkey carcass.

"Oh, no!" She burst out laughing. "No, no, no..." Marie snorted. "You couldn't possibly have thought—ha!" She dropped the knife to the carving board.

"Hey!" Mark shouted from the dining room. "Are we going to get any dinner in here, or should we all just depart and leave you two alone?"

"David," Marie said, bringing herself under control and standing to grip him by the elbows. "I'm not going to hurt you, I swear. "She found herself giggling uncontrollably. Her? A menace? Hooo.

"David," she said again, blinking hard and straightening her quivering lips. "Here's the deal."

He looked at her without flinching, his crystal blue eyes calm.

"You and I are engaged."

"Okay."

She narrowed her eyes and resisted another giggle. "You started it, I didn't."

"Okay."

"Therefore, you are mine until the night is through."

David's heart did cartwheels, but he didn't say a word.

"What I mean is, we can play this game for a few hours, just to get my family off my back. But when the clock strikes midnight..."

Holding his tongue seemed to be working so far, so why wreck it now, David reasoned.

"Then you go home."

"Got it," he said, bowing backwards as she dismissed him with a wave of her knife.

And then he darted through the swinging door and gave Johnny a high-five before Marie could rejoin them.

"More wine?" Johnny asked, passing the carafe in Marie's direction.

She'd already had two glassfuls and was thinking she should stop. But then she looked over at David holding court at the other end of the table and motioned for Johnny to fill her glass halfway.

Maybe it was the wine, or maybe it was the lateness of the hour. Or maybe, it was because she was so full of sweet potato casserole and pecan pie she couldn't think straight. But the truth of the matter was that David looked *good* sitting there in her father's chair.

He seemed so at ease with her family. And, for a man who had never met them before, it had certainly been a baptism by fire. Yet, none of it appeared to faze David at all.

"Sweetheart," he asked, looking in her direction as he stretched back and patted his belly. "Can I help you with the dishes?"

"See there," Meg said, nudging Johnny. "This man isn't domestically impaired. He's offering to help in the kitchen."

Johnny flushed and drained his wineglass. "Oh now, honey, you know I'm helpless when it comes to you ordering me around."

David knew just how Johnny felt. He got to his feet, the room turning a bit at an odd angle. Just how much wine had he had? Though he hadn't been counting, the carafe had seemed to make quite a few trips to his end of the table.

"Come on, hon," Marie said, coming over and rubbing the back of his waist.

Wow. The room came into focus then, along with all sorts of electrifying images in David's mind.

He pulled a stunned Marie into his arms. "Baby," he said, his voice husky from the wine, "you should know better than to touch me like that in public."

Someone at the table let out an amused giggle. But all Marie could see was the fire in David's eyes. It was all too clear what was on his mind.

"Maybe we should get going," Jill said, tugging on Dan's sleeve and rising from the table.

"No," Marie said, trying to break the lock of David's arms but failing miserably, "stay."

David nodded slowly as a sexy grin worked its way across his kissable lips.

Gracious! Marie thought, feeling a little sweat trickle down her cleavage beneath her too-warm dress.

"Ah, yeah," Mark said, slapping the table loudly and springing to his feet. "Time's a-wasting. We'd best all get on the road before that big storm hits."

"Storm?" Marie asked, finally wriggling free of David's embrace and practically running to the opposite end of the room.

"Yes," Meg said, as Johnny went to collect their coats from the hall closet. "Haven't you heard? They've predicted a lot of snow tonight."

"Say," Jill said, as Marie wondered what on earth she was going to do once she was left alone with David in the house, "You sure you don't want us to stay and help with the dishes? We've made quite a mess."

But David just smiled and muttered something about helping the little woman all she wanted.

Little woman, her foot! If Marie had had darts to throw, she would have aimed them straight at David.

What was wrong with her anyway? This entire fiancé thing had already gotten out of hand. There she'd sat all through the meal, envisioning David as a permanent fixture in her father's chair. And rather than her siblings, all the other seats around the table had been occupied by imaginary children—her and David's, to be exact. Six of them altogether.

She shook off an unwanted chill as David's warm hands settled on her upper arms.

"Sweetheart," he said, leaning over and kissing her fondly on the forehead, "don't you want to go and say good-bye to your brothers and sisters?"

"Of course," she said, her face the temperature—and the color, she just knew it—of stewed tomatoes.

Marie stood on the front porch and said her goodbyes, each sisterly and brotherly hug punctuated by some whispered comment about what a catch David was.

When she turned to go back in the house, David was standing in the doorway.

"How much of that did you hear?" she asked, feeling her breath stick in her throat.

"None of it..." David began.

But before Marie could get out her sigh of relief, he finished, "Except for all the good parts about what a great catch I am."

She tried to think of something witty to say, some snappy comeback that would break the heated tension of the moment. But instead her boot heel caught on a floorboard and she stumbled forward into David's arms.

"Hey," he said, shoring her up by the elbows and then tugging her in close."I think that you're quite a catch, too."

"David," Marie said, as he pulled her to him, her soft breasts pressing his pounding chest. "I think we're letting heat out."

Didn't he know it. David swooped in for a kiss, oblivious to the fact that his backside still propped open the door.

"David!" she said, stopping him in mid-approach. "My electric bill!"

David turned and looked into the house, then gave her a thousand-watt smile. "You're right, my sweet fiancée, we're burning way too many lights in there. Where do you keep the candles?"

## Chapter Twelve

Marie struck another match, wondering what on earth she was doing. But then David came up and nuzzled the back of her neck with his five o'clock stubble, and she knew exactly.

"Oh, David," she said, as little tingly kisses worked their way around the side of her neck, "you just... you just—"

"I know," he said, hungrily looking in her eyes. "You do it for me, too."

He laid his hands on either side of her glasses frames and gently tugged the turquoise wires from behind her ears.

"David," she said, her breath straining with the word. For heaven's sake, she couldn't even say his name without a million shivers racing down her spine. "I can't see a thing without those."

"Give me your hands," he said, whispering a kiss first onto one eyebrow, and then another.

Marie tightened her grip around his back.

"No," he commanded, with a fierce nibble to her neck. He raised his head and looked down into her eyes.

Even through her hazy vision, she could see him wanting her, needing her. She released her grasp and willingly surrendered her hands to his.

"What you can't see," he said, lowering her hands to the front of his jeans. "You can feel..."

Marie held her breath, as her heartbeat became a gallop.

He brought her hands around to his lean hips and held them there. "And, you can certainly hear..."

He paused and then put his mouth over hers and completely devoured her in a passionate kiss.

"Marie," he said, pulling back for a moment. "I have something very important to tell you."

And, this time, she wouldn't stop him. Because nothing in her entire life had felt so right, as she stood there holding him, unabashedly enjoying the feel of his muscular body.

"I'm glad I didn't tell you earlier, that you didn't let me," David said, his voice a low tremble. "Because then, it was only something I thought was coming..."

He pulled back his brow and swept loose strands of her hair behind her ears.

"Marie," he said, taking her chin in his hands, wanting so badly to kiss her, to dive into her sensuous fire once again—but knowing he needed to finish. "I've fallen in love with you."

She felt her knees buckle, but he lowered his strong arms and caught her around the waist, just in time.

"You look like you need to lie down," he whispered, giving her the softest kiss. "Which way is the bedroom?"

Marie didn't know what had happened to her voice, but it was gone. Or, maybe he'd scared it out of her with his sinful-as-sex, wet kisses.

He loved her? *Loved* her?

Her heart thumped loudly in response. No, it couldn't be. Not so soon after...

But then again, this felt nothing like Cecil, or Paul, or even eager Eddie, her very amorous date for the high school prom.

But, she ached in her very soul to believe this was love.

Fortunately, his safe supporting arms were still around her. "Ah... I do need to lie down."

He bent low to scoop her trembling knees into his left arm, but she stopped him with a hand on his shoulder.

"David," she said, as he straightened to look in her misty eyes. "I don't know how, I don't know why... but I've fallen in love with you, too."

Through the mist, she saw him flash a smile, and then, quicker than she could blink, she was quite literally swept off her feet and carried down the hall.

David dropped Marie onto the cushiony goosedown duvet, then straightened to loosen his belt. Though she couldn't see the details of his features, she'd captured it all picture-perfect in her mind. His ocean blue eyes, his divinely lopsided grin, his gloriously golden, manly-smelling skin...

Marie reached up and caught the front of his jeans by the waistband.

"What's this?" he asked, as she tugged him forward.

"David Lake," she said, her voice taking on a sultry quality he'd never heard. "I'm ready."

David sucked in a breath as Marie unbuttoned his pants and yanked down his fly.

"Come here, David," she said, sliding her hands down into his jeans and under the band of his briefs. "I want to see you."

David exhaled and dropped his jeans to the floor, not sure his own knees would hold up during all this excitement.

"Wow!" he said, kicking off his shoes and the rest of his jeans and springing onto the bed. "Keep talking!"

"Oh, honey," she said, purring kisses into his chest as she unbuttoned his shirt. "You haven't heard anything yet."

David fell back on the bed in wonder. Ecstasy. Excitement, as she trailed kisses down his chest, stopping at his navel to tease it a little with her tongue.

Marie didn't know what was happening, or what had overcome her. All she knew was that she wanted him, and wanted him in the worst way.

She caressed his broad chest once more, exploring the muscles there, then trailed her fingers softly, slowly down the line of his belly.

"Marie, Marie," David moaned softly. "Oh... don't stop."

He sounded positively... out of control.

She was liking this a lot. Then she straddled him and slid one hand over his hard arousal, rubbing it gently through the soft cotton of his briefs. Taking the initiative again, she pulled them off, leaving him. naked except for his open shirt.

David sat up and pressed her lightly on the shoulders. "You have me at a disadvantage," he said, kissing the top of her head.

Marie looked down at her sweater dress, wadded up around her thighs, and knew he was right. She reached for his hands and brought them to her hemline, encouraging him to help her.

In one quick move, David had lifted the dress over her head and reached for the clasp at the back of her black lace bra, as her hair cascaded down around him in waves.

"Help me," he pleaded, unable to work the clasp to his hurried satisfaction.

She reached back behind her and undid her bra, shaking it loose so her ample breasts fell freely into David's waiting hands.

"Baby," he moaned, leaning forward to lick and nibble, caress and suckle, until her panties felt damp and she knew she'd have to remove them.

Marie climbed off of him and sat on the side of the bed to remove her pantyhose and high-cut underpants.

"Come," he said, quickly shucking his shirt. He pressed her down onto the bed, "it's my turn."

She lay back on the pillows as he crouched over her in that panther-like pose she now loved so well.

"Marie," he said, lowering sensual kisses to her neck, her lips, her breasts. "I do love you, I do."

He brushed his length against her, and she felt her insides clench with a desperate yearning to know more of him.

David lowered his hips to hers, supported himself on one elbow, then used his free hand to caress her breasts once more. He lightly pinched her erect nipples and rolled them until she cried out with pleasure. Then he brought his full warm mouth down upon each, in its turn, to arouse her even more.

"David," she said, shifting her hips, "I don't think I can wait..."

That was all the encouragement he needed to lower his hands to her hips, stroke her thighs, then slip a hand in between her legs. He inserted one finger and tested the wetness there with a tender skill.

"Oh," Marie cried out, feeling her body convulse. "Oh, oh..."

David slowly withdrew his touch, and parted her thighs, positioning himself to enter her.

She gripped her hands around his naked backside and pulled him into her—hard.

He began to move in a powerfully erotic rhythm and her whole world started to dissolve.

Marie arched her hips as David caressed her breast with one hand and cupped her bottom in the other. Then he began to ride her hard and fast.

"More!" she cried out, as he tightened his grip and lowered his mouth to hers.

Their tongues tangled, their teeth nipped, and he thrust harder, over and over again, sending her to one peak after another. Marie bit his shoulder, his neck, lost in passion... until they each cried out, a deep primitive sound that united them both and sent them spiraling into bliss.

David wrapped his arms around the sex goddess snuggled against his chest. He had suspected from the start there was more to Marie than met the eye, but he'd had no way of knowing she'd respond so ardently.

"Well. That was heaven on earth. What next?"

"Dunno," she murmured. "Let's do it again."

"You're insatiable."

"If you've got a better idea, I'd like to hear it," she said sleepily.

He ruffled her already tousled hair. "You're only half awake. How about a bedtime story?"

"Hmm. Just so long as it's not *Silence In The Trees.*"

"Hell, no."

Something in his tone made Marie sit up partway, and study him for a long moment. "Wait a minute. Are you telling me you didn't like that book?"

David yanked up the sheet and buried his chin in the covers. "Guilty," he said, barely visible from his eyebrows up.

He lowered the blankets and gave a tentative smile. "Do you hate me?"

"Hate you? Oh, David! You nut," she said, giving him a playful shove. *"Silence In The Trees* was without question one of the most boring books I've ever read. But"—she stretched one long leg over his marvelously hairy calves, and snuggled closer—"I thought you liked it!"

"Well, honestly," he said, lightly caressing her arm. "It was a strain making it past Chapter Two."

"But you said—"

"No, I didn't," he said, shaking his head. "I said I thought *you'd* like it. Hey, wait a minute!"

He tilted sideways and tried to meet her eyes. "Next, you're going to tell me you don't like reading *Publishers Weekly* either."

"I don't," she said, sounding indignant. "Except, of course, when business calls for it. I'm a bookstore manager, what do you think? I read all the journals, but that doesn't have to mean they're my idea of fun."

David swatted her on the bottom through the thick layer of bedclothes. "That's my girl! I knew you had better sense than that."

He cocked one eyebrow. "You prefer that steamy stuff—"

"Romance, David. It's called romance."

"Oh, right. I really liked the part where that buxom librarian and her friendly doc were getting, uh, romantic."

Marie grabbed him by the chin and looked up. "Admit it, big boy, you liked that book, didn't you?"

"Wellll..." He drew the word out, stalling for time.

"David Lake!" she said, releasing his chin and popping his shoulder. "You were really into it... I saw you. Anyway, what *do* you like to read?"

"Well, I've got another confession," he said, ducking back under the blankets. "And this one, I don't think you're going to like as much."

He couldn't see her troubled look.

"I don't read much," his muffled voice said through the covers. "Not really." He peeped out into the darkness, expecting a verbal assault. "That is, unless you count the sports section of the newspaper."

He was sure that she'd be angry, that she'd discount him as a worthless fraud. But instead, she burst out laughing.

"Oh, David, I'm so glad."

"Glad? That I'm not well-read or—"

"David," she said, patting his chest, "I like you just the way you are." The fact that he wasn't into pretentious modern literature made him even more attractive than she'd found him to begin with. And to think, at one time she'd compared him to that unmentionable man now in New York.

David sighed and hugged her tighter. "Well, I'm glad that little mix-up with Cecil didn't do any lasting damage."

Marie wriggled out of his grasp and sat bolt upright in bed, clutching the blankets to her chest. "What mix-up? What are you talking about?"

"Well, I might as well tell you," he said, reaching over to massage her arm. "Now that we have an understanding."

She scooted over on the bed and withdrew from his reach.

"Hey," he said, his hand suspended in the darkness.

"David, tell me the truth. The whole truth, this time, about you and Cecil."

"Huh?"

"David," she said sternly, as if she were scolding a child.

"It's nothing," he said quickly. "Nothing, I swear. I didn't know the guy from Adam when I walked into the cafe looking for you. And then we got to making conversation. He, oh, brought me my coffee. I asked if he knew you, but he... what I mean is, he told me he had a way... that literary types liked him."

Marie humphed, but he continued. "Then he offered—I swear, I didn't ask—some recommendations on things I could read, an approach I could take to get a women like you interested."

"Like me, specifically?" she asked, crossing her arms in front of her.

"Holy cow... I mean, oh, boy. I mean, no, absolutely not."

She narrowed her eyes and wished she had her glasses.

"You don't think," he said, "I would have actually mentioned you by name? That I was interested, I mean? But I was. Boy, oh, boy, was I. From the moment you walked into my—"

"David," she said, unfolding her arms and crawling back over to him, "you can stop babbling now. I forgive you."

He lay there, feeling a little stunned, as she perched like a lioness and clambered on top of him.

"But I—" he said, as she began to tug down the sheet, "I just wanted a chance to explain."

"Don't worry," she said, stripping him naked on the bed. "I understand. It was natural. You figured since he was my boyfriend he'd—"

David reached up and put his hands on her shoulders. "Boyfriend?"

Marie settled her bare derriere on his thighs. "Didn't you know?" she asked innocently.

"I—uh—boyfriend? No way! When I asked you..."

"Guilty," she said, feeling anything but. "I guess we've both told our fair share of little white lies."

She looked down and spread her hands on his beautifully solid chest. He was without a doubt the handsomest man she'd known.

"Forgive me?" she asked, wriggling sensually.

"Oh, God, Marie," he said, grabbing her hips, "anything. Anything at all."

# Chapter Thirteen

Marie found her glasses in the living room and stumbled to the kitchen, tracking the appetizing scent of frying bacon. She walked to the threshold, set her glasses on her nose and paused.

*Mmm.* A blond Adonis was standing shirtless at her kitchen stove cooking up a breakfast that smelled divine.

He turned and smiled in her direction.

"Morning, wild thing. I was starting to wonder when you'd stumble out of bed."

She felt a warm sweep of color suffuse her face.

"Was I really that... wild?" she asked, tightening her robe and sidestepping to the coffeepot.

"Oh, baby," David said, coming over and drawing her into a bear hug. "Yes." He gave her a mischievous grin. "So," he said, leaning forward and giving her a hard smack on the lips, "what's your pleasure?"

"Why, David Lake," she said, looking up into his beautiful blue eyes and feeling as if she were drowning all over again, "I believe you know the answer to that."

"Yes, darling," he said, reaching behind her and playfully squeezing heir rump. "But what would you like for breakfast?"

"I... uh, coffee first," she said, still feeling foggy. Next time—and to look at him now there would certainly be a next time—she wanted to be as clear as day.

David motioned for her to sit at the breakfast table and brought her a cup of coffee. Black, just how she liked it.

"How did you know?"

"Manly intuition."

"No, I mean about the coffee," she said, hiding her blush behind her mug.

"I remembered from our coffee date."

Marie raised her brow.

"The endlessly clanking spoon."

"Oh," she said, with a giggle. She felt unnervingly silly. Like some wayward teenager who'd gotten away with doing something naughty in her parents' bed. She laughed out loud, realizing that was precisely what she'd done.

David walked over and set a plate of bacon, scrambled eggs, and toasted English muffins in front of her.

Marie brought her hands to her brilliant cheeks.

"Oh my, I don't think I've ever been cooked for before."

"Sweetheart," David said, leaning over and kissing her forehead. "Get used to it."

"But, wait! Oh my goodness..." Marie jumped to her feet, nearly upsetting the table.

"David! What time is it? I can't believe it, but I almost forgot I have to go to work!"

What couldn't she believe, Marie asked herself? That the most unforgettable man in her life had made her forget all about things like mundane responsibilities?

"Slow down there, honey," he said, pushing her back down into her chair. "Enjoy your meal. You won't be going to work or anywhere else today. Or so says local radio station WCVX."

She dropped back into her seat with a questioning look.

"Snow, Marie. The most beautiful snowfall I've seen in years. While we were heating things up last night—"

She didn't wait to hear the rest, dropping her napkin and running to the front door.

"Gracious," she said, throwing it wide. "A winter wonderland!"

A blanket of white covered the ground and delicate icicles hung from the trees, catching the color of the morning sky.

"Wanna play?" David asked, stealing up behind her and nuzzling her neck.

After breakfast they put on their coats and headed outside, and fortunately, David was the right size for Mark's old snow gear. They threw snowballs, raced circles around the big oak tree, and made snow angels on the ground when they were too tired to run anymore.

"My!" Marie said, panting as she ran back into the house. "Next time I face off against Mark and Johnny in a snowball fight, remind me to put you on my team."

"You got it," David said, laughing and peeling off his wet outer clothing. "Where shall I put these?"

"Here"—she took them—"in the dryer."

"Hmm, "David said, sneaking up behind her as she bent over the lint trap. "I've got some other parts that need warming up too."

"David Lake! Are you always this bad?" she asked without turning.

David reached forward and cupped her breasts in his hands. "Only with you."

Marie forgot all about loading the dryer and chased him back into the bedroom, where they stripped in record time and engaged in another hour-long sexual romp.

"Well!" she said, throwing herself belly down on the bed. "Now, what do we do for the rest of the afternoon?"

"How about Monopoly?" he asked, running a trailing finger down her back.

"Monopoly?" she asked with a giggle. "Are you serious?"

"Well, I like it, don't you? Sometimes when Deb and I were snowbound in Asheville, it was the only way we had to entertain ourselves."

Actually, when Marie thought about it, she and her brothers and sisters had spent an awful lot of time playing that game during the dreary winters.

"I get to be the banker!" Marie screeched, springing off the mattress and grabbing for her robe.

Hours later, they settled back in front of a blazing fire and sipped their hot cocoa.

"Today's been like a dream," Marie said.

"Yes," David answered. "Too bad the snow's melting."

She sighed heavily and rested her head against his arm. "Well, I suppose for both of us, duty calls. Your shop will be open tomorrow and so will mine."

"Uh-oh," David said, setting down his mug. "Are we getting to the part where you tell me it's time to go home?"

"Not on your life," she said, tightening her hand around his arm.

In fact, Marie realized with stunning clarity, she never wanted David to go home. Though it had been only twenty-four hours since the fiancé charade began, she was starting to realize that she didn't want to give it up. Not just the fabulous sexual attraction between them, but the other ways they related as well. David was easy to talk to, and fun-loving in a way that reminded her of her younger brothers. She'd never laughed so much with Paul, or—heaven knows—Cecil. With those two, she'd always felt as if they were observing her, just waiting somehow for the inevitable moment when she would slip up.

David, on the other hand, didn't seem to have a judgmental bone in his body. He took her for who she was and seemed to love every bit of it. What, oh what, had she done to deserve him?

"You're being awfully quiet," David said, bringing his feathery breath to her cheek.

"I was just thinking," she said into the firelight. "That other than our both hating *Silence In The Trees...*"

David chuckled.

"You and I seem to have a lot in common."

"Yeah," he said, lightly kissing her hair. "And who knows? It's only the beginning."

A beginning without an end, Marie found herself hoping.

"For example, I bet you like oldies... classic rock. Seventies and eighties, mostly."

Her eyes widened behind her glasses. "Amazing! David, how did you—"

He threw his head back with a laugh. "Studied your CD collection earlier," he said with a stealthy grin. "While you were sleeping."

She shook her head and sipped from her cocoa.

"My point is," David continued. "I like that music, too. You and I must have twenty duplicate CDs."

"Really?"

David stopped talking and seemed to scrutinize her for a moment.

"What? What's wrong?" she asked, feeling suddenly self-conscious.

"You have the cutest little mustache."

"Mustache?" She touched a finger to her upper lip.

"Made out of cocoa, right—there."

He leaned over and gave her a sweeping kiss.

"David," she said, pressing back on his chest, "if you start that all over again, I'll never get you to leave."

"That's precisely what I'm counting on." And he kissed her again.

"So, how was your extended holiday?" Caroline asked, as David bounced into the shop the next morning.

"Dandy," he said, sweeping her into his arms and swirling her across the floor. "Just dandy!"

"Uh-oh," Caroline said, breaking free and shaking out her hemline. "Something tells me that you saw Marie. And that you two shared more than turkey."

"Yeah!" David said, catching an unsuspecting Caroline off guard with an exuberant high-five.

"So, what does this mean?" Caroline asked, steadying a hand on her hip. "Is today going to be one of those wedding planner days?"

David gave a hearty laugh as Caroline blew out an exasperated breath.

"Look, with the holiday rush upon us, I can't afford to give you any more time off."

"Not even," David asked, giving her a pleading smile, "for my honeymoon?"

Marie was dreamily thumbing through a bridal magazine in the employee lounge when Joanne walked over and tapped her on the shoulder.

"If you're looking for me," she said, "I think I'm a little old—*and experienced,* "she added with a whisper, "—to be wearing white."

She looked up in surprise and then her eyes darted to Joanne's finger.

The elderly woman proudly stuck out her left hand to display a glittering solitaire.

"Oh, Joanne!" Marie said, springing to her feet and wrapping the other woman in her arms. "I can hardly believe it! After all this time... Chad?" she asked.

Joanne's cheeks turned a dusty rose.

"Took me home to meet his children. His children, Marie! Over Thanksgiving. It turned out that his grandson and I both like the Grateful Dead. I think that clinched the deal."

Marie laughed loudly and sat back in her chair.

"Sit," she said, tugging warmly at Joanne's hands. "I want to hear every thrilling detail."

## Chapter Fourteen

"Oh, David!" Marie said, racing into the optician's shop. "I'm so excited about the wedding I can't stand it!"

"Wedding?" David was going to get that little snitch. He'd wanted so badly for it to be a surprise, and Caroline had sworn she wouldn't say a word.

"Yes, it's so hard to believe after all this time!"

"Well," he said, looking over at a customer who was inspecting a display case of frames and trying to sound nonchalant. "You know what they say, when it's right, it's right."

Marie glanced quickly around the shop.

"Oh, my gosh, David," she said, bringing her hands to her flaming cheeks. "You're working! I'm so sorry. I'll come back later."

She spun and swirled for the exit.

David had never seen her move this fast. It was making him dizzy.

"Oh, honey," she said, gleefully passing through the door. "It's so exciting. So very exciting! I've got so much to do!"

David watched as Marie disappeared down the icy sidewalk, her coat caught up in a gust of wind.

The gentleman selected a pair of frames and set them loudly on the counter, his eyes traveling to the woman outdoors.

"My fiancée," David said with a tight smile and a shrug.

Since Caroline had taken the afternoon off to meet with a supplier, David used his lunch hour as an opportunity to lock up the shop and go hunt for Marie. He was sorely disappointed that Caroline had let the cat out of the bag. For once in his life, David had wanted to do it up right: wine, dinner, the romantic proposal.

Oh well, he thought, shaking off the chill that sliced through him with the wind, at least she was happy. Ecstatic, in fact. He'd never seen Marie so positively glowing. Well, almost never, he thought, with a lustful grin.

But just because she somehow knew, didn't mean they wouldn't have to talk about it. They'd have to set a date, make some plans, and—David acknowledged—no matter what she thought she knew—he'd still have to ask her officially. Get down on his knees and all that.

Besides, as the groom, David had certain responsibilities. It was his job to take care of certain details... plan the honeymoon, for example. It was right there on page three of the groom's checklist. He'd read it with his own eyes, at least a dozen times.

David strode purposefully into Books & Bistro and searched the aisles until he found her, systematically turning books cover out on the shelves so that their authors' names would be prominently displayed.

"I'm so glad I found you," he said, rushing over and giving her a tight hug.

She glanced down the aisle as if she hoped no one was looking. Well, he thought, so now it was her turn to be embarrassed.

"David! What a surprise!"

"Surprise, sweetheart?" he asked, grabbing for her once again, but she stepped backwards and bumped into a shelf. "Thought for sure you'd be expecting me."

"Well, I..." Marie brushed some imaginary crumbs off the front of her dress. "What are you doing here?" she asked, lowering her voice along with her glasses, peering at him.

"I came to discuss plans."

"Plans? Oh, David, how sweet. Joanne will be so touched."

"Joanne? I didn't know you two were that close."

"Oh, yes," Marie said. "She's like a mother to me."

"Well, then by all means—"

A customer walked over and interrupted Marie with a question. When she'd finished directing him to the New Parenting section, she turned back to David.

"So, anyway... Here's what I was thinking. It's too cold to have it outdoors. But the ceremony really shouldn't involve much fuss."

"No fuss?"

"Well, come on, now, David. Once you get to a certain age, white lace and frills do seem a little ridiculous."

She sounded like she was already putting them out to pasture. David didn't feel *that* old.

"Besides," she said, her lashes fluttering lightly behind her frames. "I think our focus should be on the part that come afterwards."

"Right," he said, stepping forward eagerly.

"David!" Marie said, halting his advance with a hand to his chest. "What's gotten into you? I'm talking about the reception."

David wiggled his eyebrows. "And I was talking about the honeymoon."

"Honeymoon?" Marie looked a little baffled. "Well, I don't think you and I need to worry about that!"

David cleared his throat. She might be walking all over him where the other arrangements were concerned, but she was not going to take the reins away from him on this. "You just go ahead and worry about everything else. I'll take care of the honeymoon."

"You? But David, you barely even know Chad and Joanne. I mean, offering to help with the wedding is one thing—"

"Chad and Joanne?"

"Of course, Chad and Joanne. Who in the world did you think we've been talking about this whole time?"

David searched his brain for a quick answer.

"Oh, I knew who we were talking about, all right," he said with a modest laugh. "It's just that I was so surprised that old Chad hadn't planned anything, I thought I might suggest—"

"Now don't go offering unsolicited advice like Cecil," she said, squaring her shoulders and closing in. "You've already seen where that sort of thing can lead."

David stepped forward and drew his arms around her waist. "Oh, I don't think things have turned out too badly in the end."

"David!" Marie said, pounding his shoulders. "I'm working!"

"Working when it comes to me, but not when it comes to planning Joanne's wedding?"

"She's a coworker, silly! For heaven's sake, it's practically company business."

David still didn't let go.

"Wait a minute," she said, finally breaking free of his grasp, "you're not wriggling out of your offer to help, are you?"

"To help with Joanne's wedding? Of course not, I meant every word I said."

"Good, because it's going to be sort of crazy between my helping with hers, and Johnny and Meg's ceremony coming up next month."

"And when will *you* get a chance to take a break?"

"Oh, I don't know," she said, running her fingers through her hair. "Unless Fabio sneaks in and steals me away to Jamaica, I'll probably be stuck here till New Year's."

Well, he wasn't exactly Fabio, but... David smiled brightly and gave her a whopping kiss on the lips. She'd just given him the most brilliant idea.

Marie tried hard not to get too concerned that she hadn't heard from David in a couple of days. After all, he'd warned her that Caroline was planning to take inventory for the rest of the week, so he'd be working long hours.

It was probably for the best anyhow. Because, as much as David had expressed his interest in helping, Marie had her hands full planning Joanne's reception. When she thought about it, she realized he would just be in the way.

The bookstore had been incredibly busy ever since it had reopened after Thanksgiving. At peak hours, the aisles were so crammed Marie often had trouble simply maneuvering to do her regular duties. The business was good for the store, as well as its employees, who would all be getting healthy bonuses this year. But the extra paperwork high-volume sales produced made additional demands on her already limited time.

Although Johnny seemed to be heading for his upcoming nuptials with a certain degree of nonchalance, his fiancée Meg was positively frantic. With only two brothers and a misguided, twice-divorced socialite mother to help her, she'd been phoning Marie almost daily for support. With the wedding less than four weeks away, the caterer had canceled, the music director had been jailed for bootlegging CDs, and the bridesmaids' dresses—all seven of them—had arrived in the wrong color!

Marie hung up the phone and collapsed in a heap on her living room sofa. Weddings were an unbelievable amount of trouble. There was so much work involved—and planning. Just look at poor Meg. She was supposed to be preparing for the most memorable day of her life, but instead she'd been biting her fingernails to the quick in nervous anticipation of what disaster would befall her next.

Somehow it seemed to Marie that the more time and planning that went into a wedding, the greater the opportunities for things to go wrong.

When she'd been little, she'd envisioned all the same things Meg had. A candlelit ceremony, followed by a sit-down dinner and dancing in a castle courtyard to an elegant string quartet.

The main problem with that picture was that Marie wasn't a princess with a courtyard, or a fortune to afford that kind of soiree. In fact, up until very recently, she didn't really imagine she'd ever find a prince.

Her sisters Jill and Teresa had found their princes early, but instead of crumpets in the castle halls, they'd been treated to tea and cake in the big reception hall of their Methodist church. To see the smiles on their faces, though, it hadn't mattered to either, not one bit.

Marie kicked off her shoes and propped her aching feet on the coffee table. What with all the circles they had to run around in prior to the big day, it was a wonder brides could dance at their own weddings at all.

No, this was too much. Too much altogether. By the time Meg and Johnny tied the knot on December twenty-eighth, Marie would have assisted with the planning of *four* weddings—Joanne's included.

She tugged the scrunchie out of her hair and shook it out as it fell to her shoulders. Gracious, she thought, straightening her curls with her fingers, maybe she'd missed her calling as a wedding coordinator.

No, scratch that. She truly enjoyed what she did for a living. What she'd enjoy even better, Marie thought, sinking low in the sofa and burying her head in her arms, would be for someone else to do everything for her when her time finally came along.

Joanne leaned in to the mirror and pinched her cheeks.

"Well, what do you think?" she asked, turning her head coyly from side to side and studying her reflection. "Not too bad for an old bird?"

"Oh, Joanne," Marie said, hugging her shoulders. "You look marvelous. Beautiful!"

It was true. One look at the glow on her face and the shine in her eyes, and anyone would swear Joanne was twenty years younger. Her hair was done in a loose upsweep with little sprigs of flowers tucked in all around. Lilac, to match her flowing, floor-length dress.

"You were so sweet to close the store, love. All on my account."

Marie chuckled. "Well, Joanne, I think it helped that your brother-in-law-to-be owns the place! But you're welcome just the same. It does seem like the perfect place for the ceremony."

"Perfect," Joanne said, smiling back at her reflection. "The scene of the crime, as Chad calls it. You know if it hadn't been for you, young lady—"

"Oh now, Joanne," Marie said, patting her affectionately on the arm. "Don't you go giving me too much credit. To look at the two of you now, there's no doubt in my mind that you and Chad would have found each other sooner or later."

Joanne turned quickly and looked at Marie. "Well, now, who on earth are you, and what have you done with my skeptical friend?"

Marie grinned and lowered her glasses. "She fell in love."

"You?" Joanne bounced on her heels like a five-year-old. "But you never said a word... How serious is it?"

"One blushing bride at a time, please," Marie said, spinning her back toward the mirror. "Now, let's be sure all those pins are in place. You wouldn't want to prick Chad when he gives you that 'I do' kiss!"

David sat nervously on the sidelines, acutely aware of what all this meant.

The back of the bookstore had been decorated to look like a wedding chapel, complete with an improvised canopy and lots of crepe paper decorations and fresh flowers. Marie had done a good job at making things look special. But then again, everything she touched seemed to have a hint of magic in it.

David hoped he was doing the right thing, and wasn't making some big blunder. But the entire family had assured him his take on the matter was perfect.

With Marie's father being gone, Johnny had been the logical one to approach. But after speaking with him,

Johnny had indicated that Mark might feel a little left out unless David also talked to him. Of course, Mark then pointed out that Jill and Teresa were Marie's sisters after all, and if—after speaking to Mark and Johnny—David somehow omitted them in the process, they'd be awfully hurt.

After all that, David had decided to sit down and have a chat with Dan and Jack as well. Oh, and he'd called Meg, in North Carolina, just to be sure his idea wouldn't upset her wedding plans in any way.

David sat at attention, as the wedding march started to play on Chad's grandson's boom box.

Marie walked in first, looking lovely in a low-cut, black sheath dress, and holding a bouquet of roses.

Then he smiled in wonder at the elegant old lady gliding down the aisle. Love, at any age, he decided, was stunning.

And he knew with a clarity beyond reason, that he and Marie would still share its glow—far past the day when their own hair turned gray.

David discreetly raised a hand to wipe away a tear as the minister stepped forward to begin the ceremony. For this would not only be a day that Chad and Joanne would remember for eternity, he was hoping... oh, how he was hoping... it'd be a landmark day for him and Marie, as well.

As the small group of guests mingled over cocktails, David turned away, searching for Marie.

"Looking for someone?" she asked, sneaking up behind him and almost startling him out of his socks.

"Marie," David nearly shouted, "don't... no," he said, halting abruptly, as her lips broke into a sensuous smile. "I take that back, surprise me all you want."

"Gracious," she said, stretching up on her toes and kissing him full force on the lips, "you're looking handsome tonight." And he did. Marie slightly narrowed her eyes, thinking she'd never seen him in a nice suit and tie before. And she liked it. Boy, did she like it.

Then again, she thought wickedly, she liked it best when he wore nothing at all.

David gave a nervous smile and looked around the room. Holy cow, was she forward tonight. Not that she couldn't be... But in public she was normally somewhat shy.

He studied her as her lips turned up in another naughty smile. "Had some champagne, dear?"

"Why, yes, I've had some champagne! And why not? We're celebrating here. Cel-e-brating! Yeee-ha!" she shouted, throwing her arms into the air and waving them.

"Marie," David said, clutching her to him and quickly scanning the room. "Maybe you shouldn't have any more."

"What do you mean, I shouldn't have any more? Hey sweet thing, why are you whispering?"

David held her even closer.

"Ouch! What are you—"

"Excuse us," David said to the very interested guests. Then he gripped Marie around the waist and carted her out of the room.

"What are you doing? I wanted to stay and enjoy the party!"

"I know you did, sweetheart," David said, bending low to grab her behind her knees. "But I've got a party of my own in mind."

"Hey, whoa!" she squealed, as he hoisted her skyward and threw her over his shoulder.

"David Lake, put me down!" she yelled, pounding his rear with her fists.

But he just pushed back the door and carried her into the night, where the December wind half froze her bare skin and sobered her up in a hurry.

"Who *are* you?" she asked, still hanging upside down.

"Just call me Fabio," he said, patting her bottom with a smile.

## Chapter Fifteen

Marie adjusted the heater vent in her direction, then folded her arms across her chest.

"I'm going to give you exactly five seconds to explain yourself, or else..."

David raised his eyebrows.

"Or else I'm calling the police."

"You mean Chad?" David tried to hold back a chuckle, but didn't quite succeed.

She huffed and looked out the window.

"Great to see you think making a spectacle of yourself is so funny."

David widened his eyes and thumbed his chest.

"Hey, wait a minute, *sweet thing*. That is what you called me in there? *Sweet*—"

"Okay, David, I get the point. So I had a little too much champagne. Well, it's been a long week. I've been working late, haven't slept much. And then with all the wedding—"

"Marie," he said, with one of those deep blue looks that made her completely lose sight of her point. "You don't have to explain yourself to me."

"Oh, good," she said, blinking, and glad—so glad— that she remembered what she'd wanted to say. "But maybe you have to explain yourself to me. I mean, what was that caveman act back there?"

David merely shrugged. "You mean you didn't like it?"

"Well, I..." The truth was, she *had* liked it. Liked it very much, darn it. It had made her feel all feminine and submissive—like a romance heroine being swept away by the masterful hero of her dreams.

"I still insist on knowing why you did that."

"I wanted to take you to dinner."

"Have you ever thought of just asking, or is that approach too ordinary?"

David smiled and lightly thumped her nose. "I guess you bring out the beast in me."

"You know," he said, resting his very warm hand on the side of her neck, "I used to be a fine, upstanding citizen. But now," he said, slipping his palm around her nape and leaning his face in toward hers, "I'm just an—animal."

Marie's eyes flashed as he drew closer. What was it that this man did to her? She tingled all over whenever he was near.

"Marie," he said, so close she could almost taste him, "the truth..."

Her nipples went hard and her body arched as all her senses recalled what David's physical truths felt like.

"Do I bring out the beast in you?"

He nibbled lightly at the base of her neck, on her earlobe... at the very tip of her chin.

*"Grrr..."* she said, latching on to his ears and pulling his mouth down on hers.

Marie pushed back in her seat and latched her seat belt.

"Are we really going to dinner," she asked, "or was that just a ploy to get me in the car and feel me up?"

David laughed and turned the ignition. The caveman routine had worked like a charm.

"No, sweetheart, no ploy. We have reservations at ten."

"Ten? Isn't that a little late for dinner?"

"As late as they'd take at the Italian Chef, but I had a hunch it might take us a while to get there."

Italian Chef? Marie's mouth watered at the thought of a rich pasta alfredo coupled with a strong Chianti... followed by a sensual night in bed with her favorite man.

"I do appreciate being taken to dinner, even if the invitation was a little heavy-handed." Her stomach growled loudly as if to accentuate her point, and they both laughed. "I haven't eaten all day."

"Marie, sweetheart," he said, lowering his voice, "you really need to take better care of yourself. Or maybe what you need"—he cast her a meaningful look but she looked away—"is someone to do the job for you."

She gripped the door handle, telling herself not to read too much between the lines.

"From where I sit," she said, trying to make light of it, "I've got plenty of people to run my life. There's Johnny and Mark—"

David started to say something, but stopped.

"What's wrong?"

"Holy cow," David said, wiping his brow with the back of his sleeve. "Talk about running things, I just zipped right through that red light!"

Marie bit her bottom lip, wondering why she'd been thinking he was such a wild man. "Wouldn't worry about it too much, David. All the police in this town are at Books & Bistro drinking champagne."

"Right," David said, sinking back in his seat with a sigh. Man, he'd have to be more careful. He needed all his wits about him tonight.

They sat face to face at the small corner table.

"I've always liked this place," Marie said, raising her glass in David's direction. "But none of my other dates," she said, her face brightening in the candle's glow, "could ever afford to bring me here."

"I'm not a rich man, Marie," David said, clinking his glass to hers. "In fact, my parents have disowned me. But I pledge to do my best to keep you in style."

Marie set down her glass.

"What do you mean, disowned you?"

"I wanted to be my own man, start my own business someday," David said. "An optician's shop. That wasn't good enough for them."

She straightened her glasses on her nose and pushed back a few locks of hair from her forehead, waiting for him to continue.

"Dad wanted me to go into the family business."

"Banking?"

"Avariciousness was more like it."

"But I thought they were well off. Didn't you say something about your mother and all her charities?"

"Oh, they were generous, in their own way. But you better believe they always knew exactly how generous they were. And everybody else did, too. Down to the last cent."

Marie reached out and laid a hand on the arm of his suit coat.

"Oh, David, I'm sorry. I didn't know it was like that— with you and your folks. Don't you even... keep in touch?"

"Sure," he said, with a wry smile, "we get together every time Debbie plans a wedding."

"Oh," Marie said, dabbing her lips with her napkin and seeming to change her mind. "Guess it's not something you want to talk about."

David brought his other hand to the table top and linked it in hers. "No, go on. I want to hear what you have to say."

"It's really not my place."

"If it were your place," he said gently, "and I asked you, would you tell me?"

"Of course," she said, unable to look away.

"Then tell me, Marie. Whatever it is that's on your mind."

"It's silly, maybe. Because I don't know Debbie at all. I mean, I'm sure that—if I did—I'd like her."

"She'd like you too," he said with a tender smile, "very much."

"Well, anyway, if your family really doesn't get along and you don't see each other much... don't you think it's possible Debbie keeps getting engaged as a way of bringing all of you together?"

David blinked and looked down at the table. It was scary, positively alarming the way she'd looked right into the situation and seen it so clearly for what it was. Of course, she had to be right. Right about his sister, right about his family.

Right on the money when it came to him.

David reached his other hand toward her, and they sat holding hands for the longest while, neither one speaking.

"I used to get sort of frustrated with the service in here," David said, slowly looking up, "but tonight I'm sort of glad for the lull. I don't know how you do it, Marie," he said, his crystal blue eyes starting to blur, "but you have a way of looking right through me, of seeing"—he brought one hand to his chest and pressed her palm to his heart—"what's in here."

Her lower lip began to tremble. He couldn't possibly be—

"Alfredo?" the waiter asked, handing over her plate.

They continued to talk throughout the delicious meal about every subject under the sun, but somehow they always came back to tonight's topic: weddings. David was regaling her with anecdotes from all the ones he'd attended and Marie listened raptly.

"Well, anyway," he went on, laughing, "until tonight, of course, that was the last wedding I went to. And after seeing the way those other groomsmen tossed poor Blake into the pool, I said never again."

"Never again, that you'd go to a wedding or be part of one?"

Marie smiled politely at the waiter as he cleared their dishes.

"Participate—as a groomsman, I mean. Hey, I was minding my own business at the bar. I had nothing to do with that let's-throw-Blake-in-the-pool-and-spray-shaving-cream-on-his-new-car business. But he was seeing double from the chlorine. To this day he holds me culpable. You try to be a nice guy..."

"And look where it gets you," she finished for him.

Yeah, he was looking. Looking right past those turquoise frames and into a soul he knew sparked with desire. She was beautiful tonight. More beautiful than ever: her upswept hair surrounding her lovely face with curls, her sleek, long neck begging for his kisses, her tastefully low-cut dress tempting him to touch...

"Well, if it matters to you," she said, bringing him back to earth with her smile. "I'm completely in your corner. I've sworn off weddings, too."

His heart sank. "Huh?" he asked, none too eloquently, reaching for his water glass with a gasp and downing it completely.

She eyed him curiously, but kept talking.

"Weddings. They're for the birds. You know, the ones who eat the rice. Such a headache, too...."

David looked around desperately for the waiter, but when he couldn't find him reached for Marie's water glass instead.

"Help yourself," she said, wrinkling up her nose. My, he was acting strange all of a sudden.

"You mean," David asked, his voice still a bit froggy, "you don't want to get married? Ever?"

Marie grabbed back her water glass and took a long sip, before setting it back down at her place.

"Who's asking?"

"I, uh..."

David turned red from the neck up.

"I am," he said, loudly clearing his throat.

She gasped at him, momentarily tongue-tied. His eyes were earnest and opened wide, his upper lip quivering.

"Marie," he said, shocking her by pushing back his chair and falling to his knees beside her. "Marry me."

Her first reaction was joy. Sheer, overwhelming joy. The man of her dreams had actually...

But then she thought of Johnny. Johnny and Meg with their own wedding three and a half weeks away.

And of all the time she'd already taken to help Joanne.

She wanted to say yes, but not right now. Find a way to keep him holding on for just a couple of more months.

But then he reached his hand into his coat pocket and pulled out an envelope.

"What's this?" she asked, as he set it down on the table before her.

"Open it," David urged. "Don't say yes or no. Just open it."

David watched her studying the envelope and held his breath. It took all his restraint not to lean over and rip it open for her.

He tried to take a mental picture to capture the moment in his mind. He'd proposed! Gone and done it! Taken the plunge headlong, and now the rest was entirely up to her.

David began a silent prayer, looking skyward.

And then, as if in answer, she fitted her nail under the seal and popped it open.

"Airline tickets?" she exclaimed, astonished. "Oh, David, that's so sweet, but—"

"Read them," he said, leveling her a look from his kneeling position.

Marie looked back down at the round-trip tickets in her hand.

"Jamaica?"

"There's something else in there," he said, still on the floor.

She narrowed her lovely eyes, then peeked into the envelope again.

"Oh, David," she gasped, pulling out a gorgeous solitaire.

David took the diamond from her hand and gently slid it onto her left ring finger.

"Marie McCloud," he said, his voice now stronger, braver, than he ever could have imagined. "Will you do me the honor of becoming my wife?" He took a very deep breath. "Let me carry you away to Jamaica where we can say our vows on a sandy beach, without the worries, the headaches..."

He gave a shaky smile as a tear broke free from the corner of his eye.

"Hey, I'll go if she won't!" someone shouted from the back of the restaurant.

"Oh, David," Marie said, leaping to her feet and pulling him up from the floor. "You make it awfully hard to say no. I do want to marry you, I do. And I love you," she said, looking deep in his eyes.

"I love you, too," he whispered back, bringing his arms around her waist and pulling her up against him.

She hardly knew whether to laugh or cry. "But I can't go to Jamaica. I can't..."

David quelled her emotion with a kiss.

"You can," he commanded firmly. "I've already arranged your vacation with your employer. We'll be back in plenty of time for your brother Johnny's wedding."

"David," she said, breathless, her helpless knees giving way. "I have obligations to meet. Deadlines... You can't just sweep in here and carry me away!"

"Watch me," he said.

And then, to a round of applause from the restaurant patrons, David swooped down and threw her over his shoulder.

## The End

## A Note from the Author

Thanks for reading *Real Romance.* I hope you enjoyed it. If you did, please help other people find this book.

1. This book is lendable, so loan it to a friend who you think might like it so that she (or he) can discover me, too.

2. Help other people find this book: write a review.

3. Sign up for my newsletter, so that that you can learn about the next book as soon as it's available. Write to GinnyBairdRomance@gmail.com with "newsletter" in the subject heading.

4. Come like my Facebook page: http://www.facebook.com/GinnyBairdRomance.

Look for my novels *How to Marry a Matador, Santa Fe Fortune* and *The Sometime Bride*, for sale in print and online as ebooks now.

Interested in seeing an extended excerpt from *The Sometime Bride?* Please keeping reading here!

# THE SOMETIME BRIDE

*Carrie swirled the ladle nervously around the near-empty punch bowl. The shower had gone off without a hitch. She and Mike—uh, Wilson—had even gotten some lovely gifts. A blender, cooking utensils. Towels. All the nice little odds and ends that help make a newlywed house a home. This wasn't such a good idea, after all. In fact, it was terrible. So many people had gone to so much time, trouble, and expense. Even Nellie's place cards were beautiful. A keepsake for the happy couple. Carrie frowned at her murky reflection centered in the twirling ice ring.*

*And to make matters worse, Mike had been an absolute champ. Everybody adored him implicitly. He'd been warm, witty, and charming the whole afternoon through. His act as her fiancé had almost even seemed real; at least his hugs and affectionate glances had seemed authentic enough. And those few unexpected kisses, though innocent enough in their placement—one at her temple, one on the back of her hand, the one at her neckline... Well, all right, maybe the one at her neck hadn't seemed quite so innocent in intent as the others. But still, no matter where his kisses had landed, each time Mike had surprised her with the warm contact of his lips, her world had caved in and her heart had let go. Let go of any notion that this thing between them was little more than make-believe. Because, though words could deceive, feelings seldom lied, and when Mike brought his flesh to hers... Carrie dropped the ladle into the punch bowl as goose bumps tore down her spine.*

*Carrie felt the hair swept from her nape. "Ready to leave?" Mike whispered, bringing his mouth close to her ear.*

*Carrie turned in surprise and found herself directly in his arms, her backside pinned against the table that held the punch bowl. "Never," she said, bringing her arms up and around his neck and pulling him in close as their lips melded in the final consummation of what they'd both been desiring all afternoon.*

*"Why don't you kids run on home?" Grandma Russell asked, blinking the dining room chandelier on and off above them.*

*Mike pulled back in a damp sweat. "Let's!" he said, giving Carrie a firm, virgin peck on the lips.*

# Chapter One

Carrie St. John strode to the edge of the pool and tugged the ring from her finger. One year, six months, and four days exactly. *Yank.* The dang thing was stuck.

Carrie looked down in frustration at the glittering diamond offset by tiny emeralds. Beautiful, yes. But— *yank*, the ring worked free of her knuckle and glided off her narrow upper finger—only a poor reminder of a relationship gone sour.

Carrie clutched her hand around the meager gems, wondering if Wilson had paid more for them, he'd have been more reluctant to leave. Hogwash, she thought, tossing back her arm and prepping for a long throw. Wilson would have left regardless. And if it hadn't been for Teresa, it would have been for someone else.

But of all the rotten things to do! Take Carrie to a scenic country inn, then drop the bomb. More like a blazing comet, Carrie thought, feeling the raw burn in her heart as she lobbed the ring forward over the water. The engagement ring pitched in a perfect arch toward the water, then plopped beneath the surface with a deafening calm.

Mike Davis ran a flat palm along the bumpy bottom surface of the pool. It had to be down here somewhere, darn it! Four months of hard-earned commission down the chlorinated drain!

If Mike had had any inkling how callous Alexia could be, he would have never gone to the trouble. Not to mention the biting expense. Now if he couldn't find the darned ring, he'd be set back financially for nothing!

Already was set back financially for nothing, Mike reminded himself, feeling his lungs drain of air. This was his third dive under and still nothing doing.

Hey, wait a minute...

Mike fishtailed over to the center of the pool where something glistened against its bottom. Yep, that was it! Had to be...

Mike swept toward the gemstone like an alligator on the prowl, then plucked the tiny ring off the pool bottom, examining it through the blurry haze caused by pool lights and chemicals. No way. But it was. Somebody else's ring entirely. The ring Mike had presented to Alexia had been a solitaire.

Despite years of high school swim-team accomplishments, Mike felt his wind quickly abating. He'd been down here too long, he realized, angling toward the surface and pressing his heels off the bottom.

Mike rocketed skyward, another woman's engagement ring clutched in his hand. Another woman who was likely just as heartless as his Alexia. When Adam gave his rib to Eve, Mike thought, breaking into the chill of the evening, the poor schmuck hadn't realized the woman had plans to barbeque it!

Carrie let out a shriek as water barreled forth and a man emerged from the center of the pool.

He shook out his honey-blond head, then paddled over to the side where Carrie stood.

"Lose something?" he asked as Carrie backed up a step.

Carrie raised a hand to her cheek and stroked back hot tears. "Where on earth did you come from?" she demanded of this Poseidon-like god, whose eyes, she noticed, were as green as the Caribbean Sea. Though she didn't know why she'd noticed, or—more importantly—why she particularly cared.

"I came from the bottom of the pool," he said, his tone not the least bit friendly. "Where I ran into a little something that might just be yours."

With that, he pulled his right hand out of the water and gingerly steadied Carrie's engagement ring between his thumb and forefinger.

Despite his hostile tone, Carrie grudgingly admitted that this swim god was actually quite attractive. Alarmingly attractive, in a way that would make most women swoon. But not Carrie, she told herself, backing up another step. Attractive meant trouble, and, in the last four hours, Carrie St. John had endured enough trouble to last a lifetime.

"I'm sorry," she said, shaking her head, "you've got the wrong girl."

Well, that was one way to look at it, Mike thought, shifting his gaze between the ring pinched in his fingers and the enigmatic woman on the pool deck.

She was dressed in a summer sundress, wavy brown hair flowing to her shoulders. Her eyes, he thought, were just as dark. Although from this angle it was pretty hard to tell.

Mike braced himself on his arms as he rose from the water.

"Don't think so," he told her, lightly shaking off and extending his hand, palm up, in her direction.

"Excuse me?" she asked, trying her best to look indignant. There was a little pout to her mouth that looked almost appealing. Almost, Mike reminded himself, not quite. Brunettes, in general, meant trouble. And Alexia had taught him that trouble not only hurt like the dickens, it was darned expensive too.

"Your ring," Mike said, stepping forward.

"You have a lot of nerve..." she said, setting her chin. Yep, Mike told himself, they were definitely brown. Chocolate-brown eyes that could probably look enticingly warm were they not so heated with vehemence.

"...intruding on my private moment!"

Mike laughed. "Intruding? But I was here first!"

She shuffled sandaled feet beneath the low hemline of her dress. Feet that were attached, Mike couldn't help but notice, to two very well-formed feminine ankles. "Well, if you were, I certainly didn't see..."

Mike arched his eyebrows, and she stopped. By the way her appreciative eyes had traveled from his damp pecs to his navel, sure as heck looked to Mike like she'd been seeing something.

"What I meant to say was—"

Mike walked forward and lifted a balled-up fist from the woman's side. "Here," he said, prying her fingers loose as she looked on with incredulity.

Mike pressed the ring into her palm. "Someone spent hard-earned money for that. Don't think it's very good of you to go throwing it away."

Carrie glared at the insolent man, wondering how he'd known exactly what she'd been doing. More puzzled still at how he dared intrude on her life. "Don't think it's very good of you to go telling a complete stranger how to run her affairs!"

"Oh, so it was only an affair, was it?" he asked, with a cool sheen to his evergreen eyes. Eyes that Carrie was quite certain could look enticing under different circumstances.

"Somehow I imagined it was a heck of a lot more serious than that."

"Well, maybe," she said, flipping over his wrist and cramming the ring back into his hand. "You ought to think of something better to do with your overactive imagination than torment women you don't even know."

Carrie turned her back on him and started toward the inn. Of all the indignities. To be trounced upon by one man during dinner, then have a hunky dish like this one serve up insults for dessert.

"Hang on!" he called, hurrying to catch up with her. "Your ring!"

"Finders, keepers," she said, picking up her pace. But what Carrie most desperately didn't want to find herself doing was falling for another man. Especially one who looked like that in a pair of swim trunks—all six foot something of virile man, dripping wet... Criminy! Carrie scurried up the cold stone steps to the main building's front door. The flame was barely extinguished on her relationship with Wilson and here she was already playing with matches!

Carrie struggled against the notion of turning back toward her predator but knew he stood silently watching her at the bottom of those stairs. Silently—rugged, handsome, yes, darn it, handsome. And wet. Carrie's throat went dry at that last thought.

"What?" she asked, spinning abruptly on her heels. "What in the world are you staring at?"

But Mike, who truthfully didn't know, just stood there dumbfounded with this beautiful stranger's ring in his hand. Beautiful, indeed. There was a fine sweep of color that just dusted her cheekbones, and somehow—given all the crying she'd apparently been doing—Mike didn't imagine it was the magic of makeup. No, there was something much more powerful going on here. Something that made absolutely zero sense. And, for a lunatic instant, Mike found himself wishing he hadn't wasted his heartfelt offering on Alexia but had given it to this goddess instead. Lunatic was right. Mike gazed up at the powdery quarter moon threading stardust through the trees, deciding he'd been out in the night air too long.

But whether he was crazy or not, Mike knew one thing and one thing only. Before she disappeared into the inn, and perhaps for eternity, he had to get her name.

"I was just wondering," he began tentatively, feeling the heat expand from his temples to the tops of his ears. "What your name is." Holy Christ. He was insane! Alexia's ring was still at the bottom of the pool, and here he was…what? Making eyes at another woman who'd just now broken some Romeo's heart?

"Why?" she asked, holding court at the top of the stairs but not looking half as menacing as she apparently intended.

"Just in case the law comes after me for stealing your ring," Mike raced in, thinking quickly. He gave her his best smile but found it impossible to tell whether she was charmed by it or not.

"Very funny."

He guessed not. "Seriously, I—"

"Name's Carrie, if you must know. Carrie St. John, and you can rest assured, uh…"

"Mike," he filled in with a grin.

"Mike," she said, clearing her throat and averting her eyes from his naked upper torso, which he'd noticed her perusing just the same. "You can rest assured I won't be calling the police on you anytime soon."

"Ah, so you do admit the ring was yours, after all."

Her eyes flashed as she turned and headed through the door.

Conniving male! They were all the same, every last one of them. And what, pray tell, did this dripping hunk of flesh plan to do with that information? Blackmail her? As if the entire world wouldn't find out soon enough. With Carrie's luck, it would make the morning edition.

Carrie let herself into her room and fell in a heap of emotion onto the bed. Her life couldn't possibly get any worse! First, Wilson brought her all the way here, to this gorgeous historic home—to tell her he's fallen in love with another woman. Then he left her, more like deserted her, in this love nest built for two, and had the gall to tell her to enjoy the rest of the weekend. His treat.

Carrie pressed her palms to her forehead to ward off her ensuing headache. But knew that it would come regardless. This was stress with a capital "S"! She'd been such a fool, had already invited six women to be her bridesmaids! And now she'd have to call each one and confess her misfortune.

And what was worse, what would truly be the worst part of all would be in facing her matchmaking grandmother. The grandmother Carrie had finally managed to convince she'd found a dashing bachelor to make "an honest woman" of her.

Carrie rolled over on the bed and clutched her pillow to her streaming cheeks. One time. Okay. But this was the second disaster she'd endured at the near-altar. What was it about her, Carrie wondered, that made men want to cut and run? Or worse still, rush straight into another woman's arms? Carrie had actually seen Teresa, knew exactly who

the woman was. And though as a fellow stockbroker of
Wilson's she certainly shared Wilson's business savvy,
Carrie truthfully didn't find Teresa that much to look at.

And that made matters all the worse, Carrie admitted
to herself, as her throat swelled tight and tears blazed trails
down her cheeks. She couldn't blame Wilson's leaving her
on something as base as hormones, or his sheer physical
attraction to another woman. No, what had caused Wilson
to leave ran deeper than that. When he'd looked beneath
the surface of his relationship with both Teresa and Carrie,
Teresa had won hands down.

Mike took another dive below the surface and cursed
himself once again for his inability to find Alexia's ring. If
she wasn't going to use it, she could have at least had the
good grace to return it, not toss it in the pool.

What was it with all the women in this place? Had they
made a silent pact to simultaneously ditch their men in this
affronting fashion? Maybe that was what this vacation
locale was all about. Some sort of fantasy dumping ground
for all disenchanted females. Bring your man to the
Sawyers House and be rid of him for good! Elegant
starlight pool, suitable for ring-tossing!

Mike was just about to call it a night when he saw
something shimmer at the far corner of the pool bottom.
Aha! It was his ring all right. One perfect solitaire that
obviously hadn't been enough to do the job. *"Marry you?"*
Alexia had scoffed. *"You can't be serious?"* Only as
serious as a heart attack, a heart attack Mike had sorely
wished he'd had rather than face the blistering look in
Alexia's cool blue eyes. *"But, sweetheart,"* she'd told him,
*"everything's been so good so far. Why would you want to
go and ruin it now?"*

Gee, call him a fool, but somehow Mike hadn't seen wanting to spend the rest of his life with someone as "ruining" things. What an idiot he'd been, believing that someone like Alexia could possibly care. Even in refusing his ring, she'd been the quintessential ice woman. Couldn't she even have pretended to have been impressed by the half-carat diamond?

Instead, when their server had arrived with dessert, she'd pushed the small velvet box aside and urged Mike to be "mature" about things. She certainly wasn't ready for that kind of commitment—and he could keep the ring.

Mike had shoved the box back in front of her, saying she could hang on to it until she felt ready. She'd given him a thin smile and said, *"Fine."* It was only because he'd followed her when she'd excused herself to the ladies' room that he'd witnessed her break the delicate ring free from its velvet prison and lob it into the pool before climbing into her black Jaguar and driving out of his life.

Just like that.

Alexia hadn't even planned to say good-bye.

Mike sat on the end of a lounge chair and studied the two rings in his hand. One glistening solitaire, the other an elegant arrangement of emeralds and diamonds. For all Mike knew, he thought, casting a tired gaze over the pool surface, there were others like these down there. Dozens, maybe. Heck, if he looked long enough, he might even find thousands.

He could start his own business: Ring Finders Unlimited. He'd make a fortune on broken hearts...

Mike blinked back the heat in his eyes and stared up at the star-speckled night, realizing just how cynical he'd become.

It was really too late to drive back to the city, and his room for the night was bought and paid for. Plus, he still had mystery woman's ring in the palm of his hand. Mike didn't know how, but some way before he left here tomorrow, he was going to get that woman to take back her ring. Then maybe she could return it properly to whoever had given it to her in the first place.

Not that it was Mike's normal style to go inserting himself in other people's relationships, but someone had to wise the female species up to the damage it was doing out there. And, since he had nothing left to lose, Mike thought, tightening his grip around his solitaire, it might as well be him.

# Chapter Two

Carrie sat at the small breakfast table, absentmindedly stirring her coffee.

"Good morning," a deep baritone echoed from above her.

Carrie looked up at the dapper man in chinos and a button-down shirt. "Mike! I almost didn't recognize you with your clothes on!"

A couple at the next table set down their grapefruit spoons and stared.

"I mean," Carrie backpedaled, perspiration sweeping her hairline, "dry." Oh, Criminy. Carrie picked up her cup, but Mike just grinned and pulled out a chair.

"Mind if I join you?" he asked.

Now that was a loaded question for eight o'clock in the morning. Carrie picked up the Style Section of the newspaper and rapidly fanned her face. "Sure, why not?" Anything, she thought. Anything to get this Greek Adonis to sit—and her to stop babbling like an idiot in this public place.

"Listen," he said, squaring his chair in with the table. "I think we got off on the wrong foot last night."

"Look, Mike," Carrie said, reaching a hand across the table to touch his arm, then instantly regretting it. It had to be over eighty degrees inside, with the air-conditioning in this antiquated building malfunctioning, and yet, still, the contact sent shivers up her spine. "As far as I'm concerned, the two of us aren't even going anywhere. So, wrong foot or no, it's all water under the bridge."

"Or, into the pool," he said with a smile that pinned her in place even though a very big part of her longed to spring from her chair and race from the room. What was it with her? What in the world was she afraid of? Mike...? And if it was terror she felt, then why did every inch of her skin vibrate with electric fire each time his sea-green eyes settled on hers?

Carrie took a very long, deliberate sip of water, then set down her glass. "You know, I never got your last name," she said with a smile she hoped looked pleasantly interested, not recklessly giddy.

"Davis," he said as a server sauntered over. "No," he told her as she tilted the silver coffee carafe, "I'm not staying."

"You're not?" Carrie asked before she could stop herself.

Mike arched one eyebrow, and the slightest tingle took hold of Carrie's tailbone. Damn it, she thought, shaking off the confusion. She was not attracted to this man, not attracted one iota. And she was going to prove it. To him— and the rest of the world, as well.

"Please," Carrie said in her most gracious Southern tone. "Do stay. It's the least I can do for..."

Their waitress colored slightly as Carrie's words fell off.

Mike accepted a cup of coffee then met Carrie's eyes with a sly smile. "You know," he whispered as their server departer. "I think you almost embarrassed that woman."

"Truth be told," Carrie admitted, taking a sip of coffee that had grown lukewarm, "I almost embarrassed myself."

Mike tore open a sugar packet and dumped the contents into his cup. "Do tell."

But Carrie didn't want to tell—tell this man any more than she had to. For, in a very big way, she already feared she'd told him way too much. Maybe not in so many words but certainly with her eyes. Guy who looked like that was bound to be experienced. Would certainly know when a woman was…what? Ogling him? Impossible. Carrie St. John was a business professional, a seasoned woman of the world. She did not ogle. She appraised. And every one of Mike's assets, darn it, were starting to add up.

"I never kiss and tell," Carrie said, realizing afterwards just how flirtatious that sounded.

Carrie flagged down the waitress and asked for another glass of water, wondering if she wouldn't be better off having the waitress dump the whole pitcher in her lap.

Mike stirred his coffee, then set aside the spoon. "Okay by me," he assured her with earnest green eyes. "Believe me, I won't be pressing you for details."

Carrie shifted in her chair, wondering why his gentlemanly assertion made her heart drop down to her belly. It wasn't that she wanted him pressing her—for details.

Criminy! She was a mess!

Carrie gratefully grabbed her refilled water and downed half the glass in one long swallow. "Won't be here for too much longer anyhow," she said, searching for a reasonable-sounding way out of the corner she'd painted herself into. "Least ways, not long enough to engage in long-winded conversation."

"I see," Mike said, studying her white-knuckled grip on her water glass. "So, then, where will you be going back to?"

"Mill Creek," she told him, feeling the room lightly spin around her. As ridiculous as it seemed, there was something about him that made her want to forget about going home altogether. Maybe it was in the heart-stopping way he looked at her, even when he pretended to be making normal conversation. Or maybe it was in the way he looked when he was half undressed…

Carrie bit into her bottom lip as Mike fell back in his chair with surprise.

"No kidding? I'm right next door in Redfields!"

"So what are you doing up here?" she asked, trying to keep her thoughts on the straight and narrow. Straight and narrow? Holy cow! Totally wrong image! What on earth was wrong with her? Never in her life had her mind been so carnally occupied!

His eyes fell to his coffee cup. "Maybe it's best if I don't kiss and tell either."

"You mean," Carrie asked with surprise, "you were here with a woman?"

He looked up, little wrinkles creasing his brow. "You find that so amazing?"

Actually, what Carrie found amazing was that any woman in her right mind who'd come here with Mike in the first place wouldn't still be here with him now. "What happened?" Carrie asked, softening her voice in concern. "I mean, certainly you don't have to tell me, but—"

"She dumped me," Mike said, bright eyes darkening. "Sayonara. Just like that. Didn't even have the courtesy to say good-bye. Simply walked out at dinner and never came back."

"No…" Carrie said, catching her breath on the unbelievable. That actually sounded worse than what had happened to her!

"Wish I could say it wasn't so," Mike said with a shake of his head, "particularly after all the… Well, never mind," he told her, fingering the rings through his pants pocket. "None of that matters much now."

Mike reached into his chinos and pulled out the pair of rings. "Not quite a matching set," he said, laying them on the table. But quite an attractive pair just the same."

Carrie blanched and looked up. "Are you telling me that... Now, wait a minute—"

Mike nodded. "Uncanny as it seems, my ring got tossed in the pool as well. Maybe it's some sort of unwritten bylaw to staying in this place."

"Only when the guys involved are first-class jerks," Carrie said with a hard edge to her voice.

A rosy band of color swept across the bridge of her nose. "Oh, sorry... Didn't mean it to—"

"So, you're assuming it was somehow my fault?" Mike asked.

"Well, it's only natural. If she felt strongly enough to throw your ring in—"

And here he'd actually been feeling sorry for her. Had been entertaining these ridiculous thoughts. Ideas that he and this fellow lovelorn soul might actually have something in common. Or maybe he'd just been deluding himself to keep his mind off his raging heartache.

Mike pushed back abruptly from the table. "Enjoy the rest of your stay," he said, dabbing his mouth with his napkin.

"Wait!" Carrie said, leaning forward across the table and attempting to grab his arm. But it was too late. He'd already laid a ten dollar bill on the table and walked away.

Carrie tipped the waitress, then hurriedly made her way out the front door. Bright sunlight spun gold through lilac bushes lining the cobblestone walk in front of her.

Overhead, morning birds called out in song as the fragrance of early summer laced the air.

This was absurd! Carrie didn't even know where in the inn he'd been staying, much less what kind of car he drove. For all she knew, he'd already gone!

Carrie looked down in a cold sweat at the two rings nestled in her damp palm. She hadn't even wanted one, and now she'd been saddled with two of them! One from a man she thought she'd known but actually didn't know at all. The other from a virtual stranger!

Carrie raced down the path, then halted where it met the gravel drive. Off to the left and down at the bottom of the grassy hill, lay the gazebo—and the swimming area.

Of course, she thought, squaring her shoulders and taking off in that direction.

Mike sat at the end of the chaise lounge, knowing it was more than just Alexia. His failings at romance had an awful lot to do with himself. Hadn't he just proven that back at the inn ten minutes ago? Fifteen minutes with a woman who didn't know him from Adam and she'd already pitched him straight into that flaming barbeque pit.

Well, fine, maybe monogamy wasn't all it was cracked up to be anyway. Just because he'd always thought he'd wanted a wife and family didn't necessarily mean that was in his cards. And every good poker player knew when to hold 'em and when to fold 'em. Maybe, at thirty-eight, it was time Mike cashed in his chips. He'd always yearned to do something different. Move to the Caymans, maybe, and open up that dive shop he'd always dreamed about.

Before, with gold-digging Alexia, he'd been reluctant to leave his "stable" job in real estate and pursue something more daring. Now, he had nothing in the world to stop him.

"Thought I'd find you down here."

Mike looked up in surprise to find Carrie standing radiant in the sunlight.

"I believe I have something of yours," she said, walking toward him and turning over his solitaire in her hand.

Mike stood. "That was awfully nice of you. But you didn't have to. Particularly after the way I—"

She gave him the soft smile he'd always known her capable of. "Didn't mean to offend you—or imply that you, personally, were any kind of jerk. That's just...uh, been my own unfortunate experience."

"Yeah, well, unfortunately, my experience with women hasn't run much better."

A cool morning breeze lifted off the water and fanned Carrie's long skirt around her legs. "We're a real pair, aren't we?" she asked, bending down to smooth out the clingy material that Mike kind of wished she'd left in place. It had been doing a spectacular job at emphasizing the curves of her luscious legs.

"A couple of losers, you mean?" he asked, wrinkling his brow. "Now, I don't think I'd go as far to say that."

"Losers, absolutely not," Carrie said, coming over and sitting in a nearby chair. "Just down on our luck a bit at the moment."

"I'll say," Mike said, pulling up another chair and sitting beside her. "Worked a good long time to buy that ring. That last house, especially, was a bear to sell. But I knew if I didn't have the commission—"

"You're in real estate?" she asked, looking amused.

"What's so surprising about that?"

"Oh nothing, really," she said, pursing her lips and looking toward the pool. "Just somehow I envisioned you in a line of work a little more—physical."

Mike spurted a laugh. "Lifeguard, you mean?" He pondered the notion of giving her mouth-to-mouth as she turned her very kissable lips toward his. Lips that had no business looking so damn inviting on such a downright disastrous morning.

Carrie shrugged two silky white shoulders that peeked out from beneath her halter-style dress. "Well, sure. That— or a rock climber. Firefighter. Policeman…"

Carrie bit her tongue, realizing how very much she sounded as if she were exercising her fantasies. And if she put her mind to it, Carrie was quite certain she could come up with one or two of those involving the well-built man beside her—clothed or not.

It was probably getting close to checkout and time for Carrie to get back to her room. Her first order of business was calling her grandmother to tell her tomorrow afternoon's bridal shower was off. It would be a sorrowful disappointment to her grandmother and all of her grandmother's old friends who'd worked so hard in the planning. Not only that, they'd all been expecting to meet the groom! And here Carrie was having to show up empty-handed.

Carrie cast a sideways glance at the man beside her, a totally absurd notion popping into her brain. No, he wouldn't. She wouldn't even dare to ask!

"You know the worst part about all of this?" Mike asked, still studying the water. But Carrie truly couldn't imagine anything worse than the look on her grandmother's face when Carrie confessed she'd let another eligible bachelor slip right through her ineffectual fingers. "It's my reunion."

"Reunion?" Carrie asked.

Mike grimaced. "High school. And for once, I thought I'd finally have a fighting chance to prove them wrong."

Carrie heaved a deep sigh, grateful that her own twentieth was still a good, safe five years away. Other than business success, she'd had nothing to show for herself at her tenth, so hadn't gone. By her twentieth, she'd been certain she'd have a dashing man—perhaps even a baby or two—on her arm. Now, she wasn't so certain.

"Which one is it?" Carrie asked, thinking she knew but feeling it only polite to ask.

"Twentieth," Mike reported with a frown. A frown that didn't much become him, Carrie decided. His was an open, expressive face meant for love and laughter. Carrie blinked hard at the thought, wondering where that love part had come from. "And the sad thing is—after all these years— I'm only going to prove those fellows right."

"Which fellows?" Carrie asked.

"The ones who voted me 'Most Likely to Remain a Bachelor'."

"Hmm."

Mike turned to look at her, his eyes catching a glint of sunshine bouncing off the spreading oaks that surrounded the pool area. They were deep-green eyes and swimming like the ocean, a deep, lulling current Carrie was quite sure she could get lost in if she wasn't very, very careful. "That's not why I proposed to Alexia, if that's what you're thinking."

"Alexia?" Carrie pondered. "Sounds very— sophisticated."

"That's a polite way to put it."

Carrie laughed. "Well, I'm sure not the most objective one to pass judgment at the moment."

"And you and yours?" Mike asked. "Mr. So-Wonderfully-Terrific you felt compelled to chuck his ring into the pool?"

"Well, I doubt I could be very objective about him either," Carrie admitted, sheepishly studying her toes through the straps of her sandals. "But then again, men like Wilson Haywood don't deserve much objectivity."

Mike cracked a grin. "Wilson, huh? Sounds very—sophisticated.

Carrie's lips pulled into a smile.

"Say," Mike began, his eyes lighting with mischief. "I've got it! How about we get your Wilson together with my—"

"Afraid it wouldn't work," Carrie said, shaking her head. "Wilson's already taken."

"That fast? That's gotta be some kind of... Oh," Mike said, his smile fading in understanding. "No wonder you chucked his ring! So tell me, what was it with this guy? Deaf, blind, or stupid? Or possibly all three?"

Carrie let loose a belly laugh, delighted with the turn this conversation had taken. "All three, I guess," she said, giggling into her hand. "And your girl? Alexis?"

"Alexia," Mike corrected.

Carrie shrugged.

"You're right," Mike agreed. "Really doesn't matter anymore now, does it? I mean, you give a gal the perfect ring..."

Carrie suddenly realized she still had Mike's ring clutched in her hand with the other. "Oh my goodness," she said, attempting to pass it over. "Here! I almost forgot!"

Mike shook his head. "Finders, keepers."

"Now, wait a minute! You left this on the table by accident!"

Mike gave her a sly wink. A wink that did terrific things for the tingles that had been lying dormant in her spine. "You quite sure of that?"

"Of course, I'm sure. You went to all the trouble to dig it out of the pool, didn't you? The ring obviously still means something to you, even if the woman you intended to wear it doesn't."

Yeah, Mike thought, that ring still meant a lot. Like about three thousand dollars, an amount he honestly couldn't afford to throw away, not with his renewed plans to move to the Caymans. If he was to make that long-lost dream a reality, he'd have to start counting every dime.

Mike stretched a reluctant hand in Carrie's direction and took back the ring.

"Quite a game of ring toss we're playing here, eh, Mike?" Carrie asked with the most compelling smile he'd seen on her face yet. Boy, wouldn't his old high school buddies just die if Mike showed up with someone like that on his arm. Classy but genuine, with an unguarded warmth that seemed to be getting hotter by the minute.

Mike wiped an arm across his moistened brow. "Got that right," he said, giving her a smile. "And it's getting a little warm out for ring toss..." Her dark eyes widened, expecting who knew what kind of proposition. "But perfect for a swim," he finished as he watched the color rush back into her face.

Yessiree, she was quite a looker. Would knock every one of that high school gang out cold! If only Mike could think up a way to take her.

"Oh no," Carrie said, scrambling to her feet. "I'm not much for swimming."

"No?" Mike asked, standing beside her. "But why in heaven's name not? It's hot as blazes out—"

Yes, damn it, Carrie could quite appropriately feel the heat. It was sticking to every inch of her with gummy fingers that prickled her skin with perspiration and sent a cascade of droplets sliding down her cleavage. But no way in Hades was she going to let a man as perfectly formed as Mike Davis see her practically naked in a swimsuit—even her modest, one-piece kind. Carrie wore her dresses ankle-length for a reason, a reason that centered mostly around her buttocks and thighs.

"Besides," Carrie added hastily, "I've got some packing to do."

"Packing?" Mike asked, looking crestfallen. "But I thought for sure you were staying. Isn't there some sort of two-night weekend minimum at this place?"

"Why yes, but—"

"Well, then, what's your hurry?"

And why, Carrie wondered, scrunching up her lips, was he trying so hard to convince her to stay? "I've got things to do," she informed him. "Arrangements to— cancel."

"And tomorrow will be too late?"

"Might be," she told him, meaning it absolutely. Too late for a lot of things. Particularly her heart. This man, Mike Davis, had an unsettling effect on her. His whole wounded-puppy-dog ploy had worked wonders at disarming her emotion. Emotion she'd sworn only last night, as she stood weeping by this same pool, she would indefinitely keep under wraps.

"Aw, come on," he coaxed with a crooked grin. "I'll bet your room's already paid for."

She looked at him and blinked. The fact was, Wilson had already footed the bill.

"Hey, I'm not proposing anything indecent here." For some reason, that admission did not make Carrie happy. "Only a little attempt at sweet revenge."

Carrie eyed him suspiciously. "Revenge how?"

"Revenge in our not letting them ruin our weekend."

Big, fat chance of that one, Carrie thought. More than her weekend had been ruined. How about her life? "Listen, Mike, it's a sweet idea, your wanting to keep me company and all…"

Now that was putting it mildly, Mike thought, feeling the rising sun beat down through his stuffy cotton shirt. Disturbingly, he was finding himself wanting to more than "keep her company." He wanted the opportunity to not even let her out of his sight—for the next twenty-four hours, at least.

The guy who'd tossed Carrie away just as cavalierly as Alexia had thrown his ring in the pool had been a total imbecile. The sweat dribbled down Mike's open shirt collar and pooled, damn it, somewhere near his navel. Without even trying, the woman set him virtually on fire. And here she was saying she was about to leave?

Carrie tapped her toe against the pool deck and considered his disappointingly not-so-indecent proposal. Forgetting the drop-dead gorgeous part, he did appear to be a very nice guy. Maybe even nice enough to be her friend. Which would be a definite first for Carrie St. John, as she'd never befriended any man for longer than thirty-six hours without things between them becoming intimate. But, of course, as her track record consisted only of two serious beaus, maybe she was being a bit hasty in making a sweeping assessment.

Besides, friendship was good. Perhaps even what she most needed at the moment. And having a friend who looked and carried himself like the athletically inclined Mike Davis, could quite possibly come in handy. Maybe even in the very near future.

"All right, I'll stay," Carrie said, "but under one condition."

"Any condition's fine with me," Mike said, knowing that as long as whatever it was involved his taking off his boiling clothes, it would be A-OK with him. Particularly if it involved Carrie St. John stripping down as well.

"You understand this thing between us is about camaraderie. Two down-and-outs on the same flip side of the coin. Compadres."

Mike gave her a tight smile, damning every inner instinct he had and telling his licentious libido to behave. "Sure thing, Carrie," he said, reaching out an arm to shake her hand. "We'll play it any way you want."

## Chapter Three

Carrie sat in the narrow oaken stairwell, finally getting a cell signal. The remoteness of the inn made service unpredictable. Carrie hadn't been able to pick up more than two bars anywhere but here.

She nervously twirled a lock of chestnut hair, rehearsing what she would tell her grandmother. *I'm sorry, Grandmother, but things just didn't work out...* No, Carrie had already been there and done that one. Besides, her second strike would make her look like a total washout, not the "together" young woman her adoring Grandma Russell took her to be.

*Grandmother, there's been a last-minute change in plans...*

Nope, that would only make her look inconsiderate. Horribly inconsiderate, given the wedding shower was scheduled for tomorrow.

Carrie sighed and hit autodial, trusting something brilliant would come to mind the instant she heard her grandmother's voice.

"Hello?"

"Grandmother, it's Carrie—"

"Oh, sweetheart," her grandma began in her endless prattle, "so lovely to hear your voice. Amelia and I were just discussing china patterns, and we really think the one you—"

"Grandmother..."

"Oh, lands sakes, child. I know, I know! Really none of my business. But, to tell you the truth, the everyday pattern you picked is ever so much more attractive and could really double for formal ware if push came to shove, and—"

Carrie blew a hard breath. This was going to be even harder than she'd imagined. "Grandmother!"

"Well, okay, okay, dear. You are absolutely right about that! Who needs to fret over china patterns when you've got a perfectly gorgeous man on your arm!"

"Grandma Russell!" Carrie shouted into the phone.

"Well, gracious me, child, you don't need to yell. Ma Bell's improved quite a bit since the days I courted your grandpa." She chuckled. "Lands sakes, child. Meant that one the other way around—quite the other way…"

Carrie sighed and slumped back against the wall behind her.

"Now, sweetheart," her grandmother finally asked, "what was it you wanted to tell me?"

Carrie racked her brain for a creative intro. "Well, it's about seating arrangements, actually."

"Tomorrow, sweetie? Your great-aunties and I've got that all worked out. No need for you to fret one bit. Nellie even hand-stitched the place cards."

The bottom dropped out of Carrie's stomach. "Aunt Nellie crocheted those beautiful lace place cards? But, I thought… That was supposed to be part of her wedding gift! I thought she was making those for the…wedding."

"Couldn't wait to see your face, she said. And you'll have to really butter her up on this one too, sweetness. She did a divine job. Absolutely divine! You would think the royal family was coming to tea, and not just your wedding party."

Carrie swallowed hard and tried to summon her courage. "Grandma…?"

"Yes, dearie?"

"What time is the shower again?"

"Land sakes, child, you are a nervous bride, aren't you? Four o'clock, same as it was last time you asked. But don't worry if you're not here right on the button. Just don't make us old gals wait too long. You know how it is with us geriatrics. We tend to nod off after a while when nothing's happening!"

"Don't worry, Grandma," Carrie said. "I promise not to put anybody to sleep."

Grandma Russell chuckled. "From what you've told me, you and that handsome groom of yours will be sure to wake up any crowd!"

"Right," Carrie agreed, feeling the fire of deceit spread from her temples to her collarbone.

"Can't wait to see what he looks like, dearie," Grandma Russell crooned into the phone. "Me and the girls have been speculating all day."

"That makes two of us," Carrie said quietly, ending the call.

"What's that?" Mike asked from the landing.

Carrie looked up, startled. "Oh, Mike, I didn't hear you come in."

"No?" he asked. "Could have sworn you said something about the two of—"

"Oh no," Carrie said with a blush. "That was my grandmother. Just got off the phone with her about..."

"Some of those plans that needed canceling?" Mike ventured.

Carrie gave him a shaky smile. "More or less."

"Say, you all right?" he asked, taking the steps two at a time and coming up to where she sat trembling at the bend in the stairs. "Because to tell you the truth, Carrie, you don't look so hot."

"Bet you say that to all the girls," she said, twisting her lips into the best imitation of a smile she could muster.

"Actually," he told her, "it's just the opposite."

"Now I see why you're not married."

Mike crossed his arms over his chest and leaned a shoulder against the wall. "This has something to do with Wilson, doesn't it?"

Carrie vehemently shook her head as moisture brimmed in her eyes.

Mike cocked his chin and scrutinized her.

"Okay," she admitted, making an inch-wide motion with her thumb and forefinger. "Maybe a little…"

Mike shook his head and held his ground.

"All right already! More than a little bit, okay? What is it exactly you want me to say?" she asked as coal-hot tears streamed down her cheeks. "That my life is a total mess? That everyone in my hometown is expecting me to show up for a bridal shower tomorrow—with my groom-to-be—and my groom-to-be has dumped me for a woman with a better financial portfolio?"

Mike dropped down on the step beside her and draped a steadying arm around her trembling shoulders.

"You don't have to be nice to me," she asserted, trying her damndest to set her jaw but failing miserably.

"I know," Mike said, reaching over and raising her chin. "But I want to be."

"But why?" Carrie asked with a sniff. "What could possibly be in it for you? I've already told you I want nothing more than…"

"Carrie, I have a question," Mike said, searching her bleary eyes.

"About what?"

"The people at this shower. Do they know...? I mean, have any of them actually met Wilson?"

"Well, only Paulette. But that was over a year ago."

"So then, she might not notice if Wilson has changed a bit? Lost some weight? Shaved his beard?"

"Lost some weight? What in the world are you talking about? Wilson was—and always will be—the ultimate bean pole! And he never had a beard!"

Carrie stared in amazement as Mike's lips curved into a devilish smile. Though, in truth, the thought had crossed her own mind once or twice—she'd never envisioned the absurd notion becoming a reality.

"Wait a minute! You couldn't possibly be thinking... That you—"

Mike nodded. "Darling, I've waited forever to meet your family."

Carrie straightened under the weight of his arm. "Very funny."

"I wasn't joking."

Carrie looked him square in the eye. "But you can't be serious! Why ever on earth would you do that for me?"

"To buy you some time?" he said, giving her shoulders a light squeeze. "Hey, I know firsthand how disorienting this type of situation can be. The last thing a nice girl like you needs is having to face her family with the abysmal news—when you alone haven't even adjusted to it yourself."

Carrie wriggled out from under his arm and set aside the cell phone. "Who says I haven't adjusted?"

Mike raised his brow and trailed a finger down her tearstained cheek. "Wild guess?"

Carrie dropped her head. "I would never accept an offer like that from a stranger." Even one who sent her stomach all aflutter like him, Carrie told herself. "Particularly not knowing you well enough to really know what you expect in return."

"No problem. I can tell you that."

Carrie looked up and arched both eyebrows.

"Class of Ninety-two."


End of excerpt from *The Sometime Bride.*
Ginny Baird thanks you for reading her work,
and hopes to hear from you soon!